OFFICER FRIENDLY

OFFICER FRIENDLY

AND OTHER STORIES

LEWIS ROBINSON

HarperCollins*Publishers*

HarperCollins books may be purchased for educational, business, or sales promotional use. For information, please write: Special Markets Department, HarperCollins Publishers Inc., 10 East 53rd Street, New York, NY 10022.

FIRST EDITION

Designed by Jackie McKee

Printed on acid-free paper

Library of Congress Cataloging-in-Publication Data

Robinson, Lewis, date.
Officer Friendly and other stories / Lewis Robinson.—1st ed.
p. cm.
Contents: The diver—Officer Friendly—The edge of the forest and the edge of the ocean—The toast—Ride—Fighting at night—Eiders—Cuxabexis, Cuxabexis—Puckheads—Seeing the world—Finches.
ISBN 0-06-051368-3 (acid-free paper)
1.Maine—Social life and customs—Fiction. I. Title.

PS3618.O33 O38 2003
813'.6—dc21   2002068816

03 04 05 06 07 ❖ /RRD 10 9 8 7 6 5 4 3 2 1

To Daniel MacArthur

[ACKNOWLEDGMENTS]

I WISH TO EXPRESS MY GRATITUDE TO THE following people for their unyielding support: Daniel Menaker; Glenn Schaeffer; my teachers; John Irving; Curtis Sittenfeld; Theo Emery; Aaron McCollough; B Love; Eric Jones; Kai Bicknell; Deirdre Faughey; Christen Kidd; David McCormick; Leslie Falk; my amazing family.

CONTENTS

OFFICER FRIENDLY

THE DIVER

Peter walked into the store in his wet bathing suit. He'd never been to Point Allison before—it was on the western edge of that remote, depressed part of Maine that didn't get much traffic. There was no one by the cash register, no one in the grocery aisles, or in the small hardware section, or behind the sandwich counter. By the back windows, though, a man with a crew cut and a brown mustache sat on a bench drinking coffee.

"I'm wondering—excuse me, I'm sorry—I need a hand," said Peter. He could feel water from his suit rolling down his legs.

"You've been out swimming," said the man.

"Can you help me?" asked Peter.

"Damn cold, isn't it?"

"Well, it's just—my wife is out there in the boat, with our baby, and we're tangled up. The propeller is all fouled."

"You need a diver," said the man.

"Exactly," said Peter.

"Tough day for it, Sunday," said the man. He had a long face with a square jaw; there was a frankness to his expression that Peter saw as vaguely canine—he looked like a spaniel.

"Divers don't work on Sunday?"

"I don't know one who does."

"Could you give me a name? I could call him and ask."

"What's your question?"

"I don't really know what to do. I have a baby out there, and my wife—she's scared." In fact, Peter was the one who'd been alarmed; Margaret was fine. Most likely she was reading her book.

"Get a price ready," said the man. "Know your price. That's what he'll be looking for."

"Price? I have no idea. Twenty-five bucks?"

"Fifty, minimum."

"Can you give me a name?" asked Peter.

"Why'd you swim in?" the man asked.

"We were stranded out there," said Peter.

"Don't have a rowboat?"

"The line came loose today. We were towing one, but we didn't notice when it came loose. I guess we lost it in the channel."

"You sure the propeller is fouled?"

"There's a huge tangle of rope around it. I saw it. I swam down."

"I know a diver."

"Could you give me his number?"

"I know a number," said the man. "What's your price?"

Peter removed a soggy mass of bills from the pocket of his bathing suit. "Well, there's sixty. My wife might have more."

"That should be fine," said the man.

"Is there a phone here?"

"I'll do it. I'll dive."

"You're a diver?"

"Not on Sundays."

Peter smiled meekly. "Could you do it, though?"

"Well, it is a Sunday, friend." He sipped his coffee, then rolled the cup back and forth in his palms.

"More than sixty?"

"Just pulling your leg," said the man. "I'll do it for fifty."

They walked side by side down the hill to the town wharf. Blackberry bushes taller than Peter flanked the dirt road. The air was clear enough to see the Matinicus Lighthouse in the far distance. At lunchtime, Peter and Margaret had sailed past the lighthouse, which was set on a small rock outcrop, five miles away from any island. Two puffins had swirled around their mast, then flown back toward the rocks, landing in the surf. It had been warm, and the baby was sleeping in the cabin below. Margaret mentioned her desire to be a lighthouse keeper; she said it was the most romantic job in the world. Peter said it would be boring and lonely and cold— it would make you go crazy. Plus, he said, all lighthouses are run automatically these days. "You're lots of fun," she said. They headed closer to the wind, tightened the sails, and as Peter steered the boat, Margaret knelt on a seat cushion and pulled off Peter's suit. "Now we're talking," Peter said. He thought of God. He thought about heaven, about dying and living forever in the clouds.

Theirs was a good marriage. They had similar interests: sailing and food and local politics and camping. They rarely disagreed. Peter felt happy and content; Margaret had long brown hair and light blue eyes; she had an athletic figure and a graceful way of carrying herself. The restaurant turned a decent enough profit and it kept their lives full. He felt close to her when they made love. There was always a part of him, though, that remained well insulated, entirely separate. This was not by plan; when she knelt there in the cockpit, for example, he looked at the top of her head, gazed out to sea, and he felt exalted but alone. He would hug her afterwards, and she smiled and kissed him. This is fine, he assured himself. It's great.

Sunlight slanted across Point Allison, catching the sides of the dozen or so lobster boats all pointed in the same direction, with their glossy hulls and radar cylinders. Peter's small sailboat faced the other way.

"I wonder which boat is yours," said the diver. "Might it be that yacht, friend?"

"That's it," said Peter. "Not much of a yacht, really."

"Bet you got cocktails out there, though."

"Sure."

"You're a lawyer?"

"No."

"Doctor?"

"We run a restaurant. We live here."

"Here?"

"In Portland."

"That's not quite here, friend," said the diver.

The diver kept his equipment in a box on the public wharf, hidden under the walkway. He stripped down to his briefs, then stepped into the neoprene suit. He was stocky; maybe he'd been a high-school football player. He smelled of tobacco and mildew and sharp, sour sweat. Peter saw himself in the diver's eyes: wearing a bright blue and yellow swimming suit, getting his propeller wound up in lines. A yachting jackass.

"You know what it looks like down there?" asked the diver.

"Not really," said Peter.

"Imagine the thickest fog you've ever seen," he said. "But it's brown."

"Polluted?"

"No, just mud. It's clean around here. Lobstermen, purse seiners, draggers, mussel farms." He grinned. "But you know what they say."

Peter shook his head.

"Clean water makes for dirty minds, and dirty minds make for lively winters," said the diver. "Or something like that." He laughed with shiny white teeth.

"Many fish down there?" asked Peter. Once he'd said it, it seemed like just the kind of question a jackass yachtsman would ask.

The diver pulled the wet suit hood down over his head and zipped the jacket. "Plenty. They're hard to see, though. They sneak up on you. You know what a sculpin looks like? They come out of nowhere. They're covered in sharp spines with big bulging eyes and huge rubbery mouths." He opened his eyes wide and stuck out his lower lip, then laughed at himself. His neck strained; it was broad and muscular.

"You must see lobsters down there, too."

"Oh, they're like cockroaches. They're everywhere. And they eat anything, garbage and dead fish. They eat their brothers, too, like cannibals." He smiled and strapped a knife to his leg.

"What's that for?" asked Peter.

"Say you get your hoses tangled in kelp. Or a shark comes at you." The diver took the knife out of its sheath and wiped off the blade, then, to test its sharpness, scraped it on his palm.

"Shark?"

"Come on, friend," said the diver. "Joke."

"Oh," said Peter. "Right."

"The seals here bite, though."

"Seals?"

"Jesus, you're gullible. Where'd you say you're from again?"

"We live in Portland."

"Where's that?" asked the diver.

Peter looked at him. Then he forced out a laugh.

"You almost thought I was that dumb," said the diver. "I'm pretty dumb, but I know where Portland is. I may not run a fancy restaurant, but I know where the city is, friend." He attached the hoses to his tank, then hefted it all to his back and clipped himself in. "Grab me those flippers, will you?"

Peter grabbed them and handed them to the diver. "You're my diving buddy, friend," the diver said. "Don't let me sink."

The diver fell in backwards, which made the tank slap hard

against the water. Peter dove in. He hated to swim; he was slow, and being in the water—having to swim a distance, slowly—made him feel weak. He was looking forward to warm food. The diver put his hands behind his head and flippered along on his back, powering himself out to the boat, and bobbed there, waiting.

Margaret set out the swimming ladder, leaning over the side, wearing a green bathing suit under an unbuttoned dress shirt. Her cheeks were flushed from wine; her hair hung on her shoulders and fell across her face.

"Cold?" she asked, smiling.

"Freezing," said Peter. He climbed the ladder and she wrapped him in a towel the size of a picnic blanket.

"Oh, come on. It's toasty. You got to toughen up, friend," said the diver. He looked up at Margaret and said, "Hello, dearie." She nodded back at him. He unsheathed his knife and set it between his teeth, clutching it there like a pirate. "Arrrrr," he said. Margaret put her arm around Peter and laughed. Then the diver grabbed the knife with his neoprene mitt and said, "I'll go take a look. If I don't come up in a few minutes, you better come down and get me." He put the regulator in his mouth and submerged. Foot-wide bubbles broke the surface.

"What a creep," said Peter.

"He seems harmless," said Margaret.

"He really played me up there. He got me to count my money before he told me he was a diver."

"Shush," she said. "Just look at how beautiful this place is."

They'd never been as far up the coast—the spruce forest

was dark purple; the low sun cast yellow light against the small clapboard houses. The wind was dying and the water was black. Breezes swept across the harbor, ruffling the glaze.

She put her hands on Peter's neck, and when she kissed him he could taste the wine; she pressed into him and he moved his hand to the top of her swimsuit, easing it down and kissing the top of her breast.

He nodded toward the cabin. "Is Chloe sleeping?"

"She hasn't peeped since we arrived."

"Will you promise me something?" asked Peter.

"Yes?"

"Just promise me you won't invite this guy for dinner, okay?"

"Why would I do that?"

"Because you do that. You know you do. You get caught up and next thing, we've got Jehovah Witnesses in our living room."

"Oh, please," said Margaret. "They were sweet. And it was February and they'd been walking around for hours."

"Just promise," said Peter.

"They were Mormons, by the way."

He wanted as much time alone with her as possible; he wanted to break through the lonely feeling he'd been having, and the sailing trip had been in his mind for a long time. He knew it would be good for them.

He glanced over the side. "How long has he been down there?" he asked. He moved to the rail, a cable sheathed in rubber, and looked over. There weren't any bubbles. He stepped to the starboard side, and there, too, the water was flat.

"Damn," he said. He dropped the towel and dove in.

The cold tightened his skin, making it hard to hold his breath, and when he opened his eyes, they stung. It was hazy and quiet. The basketball-sized mess of rope on the shaft was gone—the silver propeller was in clear view, but not the diver. Looking down, he saw shafts of sunlight through tendrils of algae, which faded to darkness. He came up for a breath, then swam for the bottom, kicking hard, clearing his ears, pulling at the water with his arms. It got darker, and his hands scratched the mud, and everything clouded; he thought he saw the antennae of a lobster, and maybe the flash of a claw, then the mud blinded him. He puffed his cheeks and surfaced. Margaret hung over the side. Peter coughed. "I didn't see him," he said.

Peter climbed the swimming ladder, shivering, and he looked at the lobster boats, then looked out toward the woods. The diver was standing on the shore, like a man on the moon. He waved at Peter and Margaret in a long slow arc over his head. "Ahoy!" he yelled. "You must really love it in that water, friend. Ha!"

"For Christ's sake," muttered Peter.

"Oh, look at that," Margaret said, laughing. "He was all the way over there."

"Fire up your stove," the diver yelled again. "I'm bringing mussels." He was stuffing them in the pockets of his inflatable vest.

Peter put a finger up to his lips. "Shhhh," he said in a whisper. "The baby's sleeping. We can't cook now."

"I don't think he can hear you," said Margaret.

"What?" shouted the diver.

Chloe cried from below. Margaret stepped into the cabin. The diver made his slow approach through the water, casting a gentle wake. When he got close, he raised his head. "You get bit by a seal down there, friend?" He gripped the ladder.

"Wasn't I supposed to come and get you after a few minutes?" asked Peter.

"You got to know when I'm joking, friend."

"How much do I owe you?" said Peter.

"Aw, don't worry about it. I'm having fun," he said. "Let's say half price. Just give me a hand with this tank, will you, friend?"

"Shouldn't you try getting back across? It's almost dark."

"Friend, this harbor's like my wife's ass. I can feel my way around it in the dark." He raised his eyebrows.

Peter forced a smile. That afternoon on the quiet ocean, after they'd passed the lighthouse, he'd spent a few hours thinking about absolutely nothing, no concerns about the restaurant, nothing. Just peace. Margaret was nestled against him, sleeping. The sky and the wind were perfect. The only sound was the hull of the boat moving through the waves. He felt alive and settled. And now he was in Point Allison, dealing with this jerk. He just wanted to get the guy out of his sight.

"You like that one, Peter? Thinking about my wife's ass?"

Peter said, "Frankly, I'd rather think about my own wife's ass."

"Me, too," said the diver.

"Excuse me?"

"I'm thinking about your wife's ass," said the diver. "Round as the moon." He raised his eyebrows. Then he slipped out of the tank's shoulder straps. "Just kidding, friend! Wow, you're a gullible mother. Here, take the tank."

Peter looked at the diver, who had pushed his mask up on his forehead. His eyes were big and brown, and his mustache dripped. His fins floated beside him. Smiling, he held the tank up toward Peter. They stared at each other.

"Maybe you should head back now," said Peter.

The diver stopped smiling. "I'll unload the mussels," he said. "And then you can pay me."

"I think we're all set for food," said Peter.

"Don't get me wrong," whispered the diver. "I'm really dead serious about that ass. It's fantastic. You got to take my word—I'd kill for ass like that. You're a lucky man, friend."

Peter reached for the tank. He took it by the nozzle, heaved it up toward the rail. Now he felt better, in charge. The tank was lighter than he expected, but it was still a good weight, perhaps twenty pounds. What crossed his mind—it was a strong, momentary urge—was to punish the man. The diver looked up and stepped on the swimming ladder, and Peter let the tank fall against the diver's head. It fell nearly a foot, and though it didn't hit him squarely—it glanced off his temple, which was covered by the neoprene hood—he'd known he hurt the man. The diver slipped from the ladder, went under, then corked to the surface. His face was submerged with small bubbles spritzing around the mask.

Peter looked at the top of the diver's head. Then he set the tank on deck and jumped in the water. He grabbed the diver from behind, and with one hand on the ladder, held the man's face above water.

Chloe had stopped crying and the harbor was silent. Peter's ears rang. He swept a look around, at the lobster boats, at the clapboard houses now gray in dusk, at a black-backed gull perched on a green navigational marker in the center of the harbor. With two strong flaps, the bird was up and flying toward the town wharf. It called twice—squawk! squawk!—then everything was still again, and Peter's breath was loud as he treaded water with the slumped diver in his arms. The diver's head drooped and his mouth hung open. Peter wondered if he was dead.

Peter hitched a strap from the diver's suit to the side of the ladder, then climbed into the boat. With his chest against the deck, Peter grabbed the diver under the arms and pulled up. He had the diver's head above deck when Margaret came out of the cabin, wearing jeans and a sweater.

She hesitated on the steps. "Peter?"

"Grab the back of his suit, will you?" said Peter.

"Is he okay?"

"He's out," said Peter.

"What happened?"

"He hit his head on the tank."

"Ouch," she said.

"Ouch is right," said Peter. "It knocked him out."

They laid him on the plastic bench cushion in the cockpit. Peter kneeled and pulled off the diver's hood, then put his hand in front of the diver's nose, felt his hot breath. This relieved him somewhat, but it startled him, too. Then he slapped the side of the diver's face lightly. He pried open one of the diver's eyelids, and the eye looked dark and empty. Peter grabbed the diver and shook him. "Wake up, wake up," he said.

"We should roll him on his side, in case he starts throwing up," said Margaret.

Peter rolled him on his side. "Wake up," he said. With his thumbs, Peter pulled open both of the diver's eyelids. Now they were rolled up in his head, so all Peter could see were the whites. Peter let go of the eyelids and they fell shut.

"What does that mean?" asked Peter.

"I don't know," said Margaret.

"Pinch me," said the diver.

Peter jumped back against his wife.

"Pinch me to see if that'll work. Pinch my nose," said the diver. He started to laugh. "Pull my finger," he said. He kept his eyes shut but offered his pointer finger to Peter.

"Jesus," said Peter. "Are you okay?"

"Doing great," said the diver. "It conked me a little bit, but I just wanted to get you in the water again, Peter. Ha! You were scared, weren't you, friend?"

Peter exhaled. He took Margaret's arms and wrapped them around his chest. "God," he said. "Wow."

"You got a pot of water on?" asked the diver.

"I'll see if it's boiling," said Margaret. "Should I get you some ice?"

"For my head? No," said the diver. "But I'd love some with

my rum. Rum on the rocks, the drink of admirals. You have some rum?"

"You sure that's the right thing to be drinking after bumping your head?" asked Margaret.

"It's the perfect thing," said the diver.

"I'll make you a light one," said Margaret. She went below.

"Peter," said the diver. "Friend. Come sit by me. I've got something to talk to you about."

Peter's stomach felt queasy, and his legs were cold. He wrapped himself in the towel and moved next to the diver.

Margaret yelled up from below, "Can I get you some dry clothes?"

"Oh, lovely," the diver yelled back.

Margaret popped her head out of the cabin. "It's okay, Peter? He can use your sweat suit?"

"Fine," said Peter. Margaret returned below.

The diver draped his arm over Peter's shoulder. "Friend," whispered the diver. "You told your wife I hit my head on the tank."

"That's right."

"That I hit my head on it," said the diver.

"It must have slipped," said Peter. "Sorry about that."

"You're sorry?" asked the diver, smiling. He pulled Peter in close. "Friend, you tried to kill me."

"No," said Peter. "That's a heavy tank. It slipped."

"You tried to dash my brains out," the diver whispered. "You got angry, friend." He smiled again. Margaret came into the cockpit with a tray holding three glasses and a block of white cheese with thin crackers. She had the sweat suit and a towel wedged under her arm.

"We're so glad you're okay," said Margaret.

"You're a doll," said the diver, taking his drink. "I have something I'd like to say."

Margaret picked up her glass. Peter felt exhausted. When he raised his glass, it was heavy in his weak hand. The evening was all wrong; the smile the diver wore—like a dog's smile— did not bode well.

"To the beauty of truth, and the truth of beauty," the diver said, winking at Margaret. She laughed and looked at Peter. They clinked their glasses together. "Welcome to Point Allison," the diver continued, swallowing half the rum and setting the drink down. He unfastened the knife from his leg and laid it next to his drink, then unzipped the front of his suit. He peeled it off his shoulders, stood up, and took it down to his ankles. The thick neoprene squeaked when he pulled his feet out. His smell was less sour; he was salty. The sun had just dipped below the islands, and in the faint light the diver's skin was dark red and steaming.

"Toss me that towel, doll." He put out his hand toward Margaret, smiling there in his skivvies. He turned his back to them, dropped his drawers, toweled off, and stepped into Peter's green sweat suit. He zipped the top of the outfit all the way to his chin. It was tight on him, accentuating the width of his chest.

"Ahhh," he said. "Great. Fantastic. If the peasants could only see me now." He picked up his rum and drank it down.

"Peter, would you take the mussels below and put them in?" Margaret said. "And check on Chloe, would you?" She sat back against a deck cushion, putting her feet up.

"I'm too cold to move," he said.

"Then go get some clothes, silly," she said.

He looked at the diver, who nodded in agreement. "Don't mind us. You're excused," said the diver.

"I'm really . . . I'm aching. Let me just rest here for a minute, okay?"

"I'll go," she said. "Peter, you can be so lazy." She said this jokingly, but he could tell she was annoyed. She gathered the mussels from the diver's vest.

When she left, the diver put his arm around Peter again. "You're a liar," he said. "They should lock you up."

"That's absurd," whispered Peter. "What are you talking about?"

"Your pretty wife, she doesn't know the real you, does she."

This was not worth answering; the diver knew nothing about Peter. Nothing. Peter loved his wife, and she loved him. That was clear. He so wanted to be alone with her now. He'd dropped the tank mostly by mistake, perhaps slightly out of anger. He wouldn't let the diver bully him. What proof did he have of anything? He just needed to get the guy off his boat, and everything would be fine. Tomorrow they'd be sailing in the sun again.

Margaret came halfway up from the cabin and tossed Peter a sweater and jeans, then returned to the stove.

"Thanks, honey," he called after her. He wrapped the towel high on his waist and changed pants underneath it.

"You must not be used to hospitality," said the diver. He unsheathed the knife and held it gingerly, letting the handle roll in his hand. The blade reflected the orange bilge light on a neighboring lobster boat. "Diving for you on a Sunday. Bringing you mussels. This is Point Allison hospitality. And now you're not talking to me, like a rude bastard."

"I didn't ask for anything," whispered Peter.

"Sure you did," he said. "Besides, you shouldn't have to ask for hospitality, friend."

"Please stop calling me that," said Peter.

"Friend, I'm the one back from the dead, remember? I'm the boss." With his knife, the diver scratched salt off the back of his hand. "Here's a question," said the diver. "Do you think you're a better man than me?"

"No," said Peter.

"Which means yes, right?" said the diver.

"It means no," said Peter.

"Let's make a deal," said the diver. He sheathed the knife. "You stay here, be the town diver. I'll sail back to Portland, run the restaurant and have your wife."

Peter laughed. "No deal," he said.

"What's so funny?" asked the diver. "It seems like a good deal to me. You'd like it here. It'd be good for a guy like you."

"Not a chance."

"I know your type. You like things simple. You can keep to yourself here. No one has to know what a liar you are."

"You wouldn't know what to do with my restaurant, pal. Or with my wife."

"Oh, I have a few ideas, friend," said the diver.

Margaret returned to the cockpit with a tray of steaming mussels. She'd put candles in the center.

"Voilà," she said.

"Beautiful," said the diver.

"How's it going up here?" she asked.

"You know, Margaret," said the diver, smiling and patting Peter on the back, "your husband and I have gotten right to the heart of things, right away. It's a rare thing. Like he was my brother or something. It's very pleasant."

Margaret said, "Well, I'm glad." Then she looked at Peter. "Honey, are you okay?"

"Fine," he said.

They ate the mussels quietly. Peter ate very slowly; he wasn't hungry at all, but he didn't want to draw attention. The mussels slipped down his throat. The diver tucked a napkin into the top of the sweat suit.

"These are excellent," said the diver, dabbing the corners of his mouth with the napkin.

"They're a specialty at the restaurant," said Margaret. "Did Peter tell you about the restaurant?"

"He certainly did," said the diver.

"Oh, look at your head!" said Margaret. She scooted closer to the diver. "Let me see." He smiled and lowered his head, putting his chin to his chest. There was a tablespoon-sized bump near his temple, just above the hairline.

"Someone should take a look at that," said Margaret. "And check your pupils, too."

"But we're just getting started," said the diver. He licked his fingers.

"Now that the propeller's free, we can take you to the wharf," said Peter.

"Pour me a spot more of that rum, will you, doll?" asked the diver.

When Peter started the engine, he knew it would seem abrupt—Margaret looked at him quizzically—but he was now ready to take charge of the evening. To hell with the diver. The moon hadn't risen, so the water was difficult to distinguish from the air, but a yellow light glowed in the distance. Chloe was crying again, startled by the engine. Margaret brought her to the cockpit just as Peter hauled the anchor.

"What a beautiful, beautiful child," said the diver. "I think she's got your eyes, Peter."

Peter was steering, and he looked at Chloe, but she was too dark to see clearly. "They're bluish, more like Margaret's," said Peter. "Are we going in the right direction?"

"Head for that light," said the diver. "That's the wharf."

"Would you like to hold her?" asked Margaret.

"Love to," said the diver.

"I say let's not pass her around right now," said Peter.

Margaret hummed to Chloe and rocked her back and forth. They approached the float with the diesel engine at its lowest idle. Peter clicked it into neutral, and it rumbled there, an exhaust valve splashing water out the stern. Peter jumped to the wharf and fastened a line.

The diver stretched his arms out to Margaret and Chloe. "Let me see that little sweetie," he said.

"She's so quiet now. Let's not startle her," said Peter. He caught the diver's eyes.

"Oh, I've got a great touch," said the diver. "Just a look, then I'll be on my way."

Peter watched as Margaret passed Chloe to the diver, who held the baby against his chest and hummed to her as Margaret had. It was the only sound in all of Point Allison. "So perfect," he said, gently handing the baby back to Margaret, who took her down below. He unloaded his equipment, stepped to the wharf, and unzipped the front of the sweat suit, starting to pull it off his shoulders.

"Keep it," said Peter. "And here's your pay." Peter took a ten and two twenties out of his wallet and folded them in half, handing them to the diver.

"On the house," said the diver.

"Take the money," said Peter.

The diver bent down and came up with the knife, un-sheathed.

"Here's a souvenir," he said. He offered Peter the knife, handle forward. The diver stood still and waited for Peter to take it. "Go ahead. It'll remind you of me, friend," he said. "Just like I can wear this sweat suit and remember our good times." He held the handle toward Peter with a blank face.

"We should get going, now," said Peter.

"It's a gift. I'm giving you something," said the diver. "Take it."

"No, thanks," said Peter, but he knew if he took the knife, it would all be over. He returned the money to his wallet. When he grasped the handle, the diver released the blade gently, and Peter set the knife on the seat cushion beside him.

"I'll be seeing you, friend," said the diver, smiling.

Margaret returned to the cockpit to say goodbye. "Thanks for the mussels," she said. "They were lovely."

"As were you," said the diver. "By the way," he continued. "There's something you should know about your husband."

"What's that?" she asked.

Peter untied the lines; in minutes, they'd be in the quiet of the night, sailing out of Point Allison.

"He's a top-notch guy. You're lucky to know him."

"Of course," said Margaret.

The diver waved as they motored away.

Later, they snuggled together while Peter steered. With a flashlight, Margaret consulted the chart and made sure they were sticking to the channel, that there was plenty of water beneath them. In an hour, the moon came up behind them, giving the waves shape in the dark.

When Chloe started to cry, Margaret went below.

Peter felt exhilarated, reborn. He found the knife on the seat cushion beside him and flung it off the stern. In the moonlight, he saw a splash and imagined the knife's winding path to the floor of the ocean.

OFFICER FRIENDLY

ZIEGLER WAS INTO CHEAP THRILLS, LIKE ME, AND CARED only about not getting caught. We had this routine which involved going to the J.M. Biggies parking lot and sending bottle rockets over the road. Cars often stopped but we hid behind J.M. Biggies' dumpsters so people couldn't find us. One night a cop came into the parking lot at full speed without his lights on. This startled us. We started running. On the rink in skates I was quicker than Ziegler but on foot he had me. The cop spun to a stop in the snow and hopped out, like a pro. He hoofed it after us. Ziegler hit the snowbank just as the cop yelled "Freeze!"

I couldn't believe it. He actually yelled "Freeze!" as though he was in charge of the situation. We knew all the cops in Point Allison. They were subpar. This one yells "Freeze!" just as Ziegler is getting over the snowbank. I'm still running, and I'm thinking, This chump's going to shoot me. Shoot me dead for sending up bottle rockets. Sixteen years alive and I was going to get shot in the back by a Point Allison cop. The local force was generally incompetent but capable of occasional displays of accidental heroism. So I stopped, and the cop kept running, and just as I turned around he tackled me in the snowbank.

I'll hand it to the guy: it was a great takedown, executed cleanly, powerfully. In fact, the enthusiasm of the tackle sent his fur hat to the top of the snowbank. He held me and caught his breath. He was wheezing and his warm stomach was pressed against my chest.

"Don't . . ." he said, but then he had to catch his breath and start again. "Don't . . . ever . . . run . . . from . . . an officer . . . of . . . the law."

His nose was inches from my forehead. It was Officer Friendly, the cop who in fifth grade had visited our classroom to write the word DRUGS on the chalkboard. Later in his speech, .e crossed the word out, and later still, he erased it. This routine was mimicked by many of us in the years that followed.

When he put his hands on the snow on either side of me to push himself up, his arms sunk in and he was pinning me again. I was pressed deeper into the snowbank.

"Just a minute," he said.

"No problem," I said.

IN HIS SQUAD CAR, WE SAT IN SILENCE NEAR THE SIDEWALK on Main Street. He idled the engine and set the heat at full blast, the blowers on our faces, and I wondered if he was trying to compose what he was going to say, or if his strategy was more fine-tuned, if in fact the silence was his way of trying to scare me, trying to get me to realize the gravity of the situation, the detriment of firecrackers. His breath was loud because he pushed it through his teeth. Aside from his gig as Officer Friendly, he patrolled the hockey games; I'd seen him standing by the entrance before the puck dropped, and once the action started he'd go up into the bleachers. His name tag said Belliveau. He looked my dad's age.

"You know what running does?" he asked.

I chose not to answer. It was obviously a trap. I almost said, Well, running got my buddy up and over the snowbank so he didn't have to get pinned by you in the snow, but I resisted.

"What running does, my friend, is that it makes you look like a real criminal," he said. "My guess is that you're not a real criminal. Why would you want me to think you're a real criminal?"

I suppose I didn't want to look like a criminal but I was annoyed that my jean jacket, black wool hat, and steel-toed boots didn't speak danger. Belliveau obviously didn't know the half of it.

"There are a lot of things you could have been doing back there," he said. "For all I know, you could have been using a controlled substance. I could go right down the list. Assault, vandalism, kidnapping, arson. The people who run away are the people who are doing the worst things. That makes sense to you, doesn't it, son?"

"Of course, sir," I said. But I was thinking: Right, Officer Friendly, okay, you're an idiot. That guy who got over the snowbank? I was kidnapping him, and now he's gotten away.

"What's your name, son?" he asked. There were dark stains under his arms and down the middle of his chest. He switched the heat to defrost. He'd done his share of good cop, now he'd go to bad cop. I knew the whole shtick.

"Charlie . . . Pinkie," I said.

"Pinkie. Huh. Haven't heard that name. Maybe you have some identification, Mr. Pinkie? Curious how you spell 'Pinkie.' If it's with a *y* or an *i-e* or *e-y*. Or is it double *e*?

Officer Friendly was getting cute on me. I didn't like that. It was common, though, among Point Allison cops. Ziegler and I would walk across the snowpack in front of the high school late at night and the cops would roll by slowly, then turn around even slower, so you could hear the squeal of the power steering and ice snapping under their tires. We loved it when they used the cruiser's loudspeaker. "HEY, YOU, UP BY THE SCHOOL."

This always made me shiver, in the good way—like when I saw myself on TV for the first time, Channel Six sports high-lights, the Lewiston game. I was skating up the boards, and I was only on for a flash, but it was definitely me, in the blue hel-met, right there on Channel Six.

"COME OVER HERE," they'd say into the loudspeaker, or better yet, "DROP TO THE GROUND."

They lowered their windows electronically; they clicked on their mag lights and shined them in our eyes. And all of them, every one, used that cute tone. Even Officer Friendly: full-guns cute.

"I don't have my wallet with me," I said.

"Mr. Pinkie doesn't have his wallet," he said, staring straight ahead. He adjusted himself. "What do you say I recognize you? That I know you play hockey with my son? I can make one quick call to dispatch, I find out exactly who you are. Find out exactly who your folks are. How about if I call them up? Tell them where you're at, that you're sitting here with me?"

So Belliveau had some moves. But I could call his bluff. There was no Belliveau on my hockey team. "Edward Mc-France," I said. "My friends call me Eddie."

He picked up his police radio and said, "Joyce, patch me through to home, will you? Thanks."

The sound of a phone ringing came over the radio, and then someone picked up.

"Hello?" said the voice.

"Johnny, who's that kid on your team with the bad attitude, the one who scored the second goal on Sunday—he was in the crease but the ref didn't see it—you know, he put up his arms like he had just won the gold medal?"

"Jake Ritchie," the voice said.

"And who's his buddy?"

"Travis Ziegler."

"Okay, thanks, Johnny."

Johnny fucking Anderson. Damn. His mom marries a cop, and just like that he's an informant. Coach had a drill and Johnny fucking Anderson always had it in for me. Coach called the drill "battle chops." He'd select one of us to be the "war dog" and another to be the "gunner." Then he'd pick up a puck and throw it to the far corner of the ice, where it would slap and bounce its way to the boards. With a nod, Coach would send out the war dog, wait a few beats, and with a second nod, send in the gunner. Johnny Anderson always seemed to be my gunner. He'd catch me with his stick right under the shoulder blades, and when I bent over from the hit, he'd spear me in the gut. But Ziegler was Johnny's gunner once, and he dropped Johnny to the ice with a knee to the kidneys. I thought it was great. In fact, I laughed my ass off.

Belliveau took a small notepad from his chest pocket and clicked his pen against it. "Mr. Jake Ritchie, now I've got your name. And your friend Travis. You guys are on my list. You know about my list?"

I looked over and saw that he had spelled my name wrong and butchered Ziegler's. We were the only two names on the page. Then he wrote, in parentheses: Charlie Pinkie, Eddie McFrance.

"No, sir, I don't, sir," I said.

"Mr. Ritchie, don't be smart with me. Fleeing the scene, false impersonation. You deserve more than being on my list, not that being on my list is any small shake. This list goes to all the other cops, and if they catch you doing anything stupid—which is a long shot, right?—you'll be talking to me again, and it won't be anything like this."

Then he gave me more silence. There were no cars on the street. Where there wasn't snow, there was sand and ice. I looked down the street, toward Stegger's package store—Stegger had closed up hours ago, but he kept his fluorescents on. I looked back up the other way and saw an old man, stooped over, in a full-length trench coat. His movement down the sidewalk was so slow that it was barely noticeable.

Belliveau watched the old man as he neared the cruiser's headlights. I'll agree that the guy was something worth staring at. Every step he took was hesitant, like a robot, and he was hunched so far over and had his hat pulled so far down that you couldn't see his face. He was shaking everywhere. He looked about a hundred years old. He must have really needed to get to Stegger's, and he must not have known that Stegger's was closed. It was 1 A.M. and well below freezing.

We were parked close enough to the sidewalk so that when the old man got in the beam of the headlights—and these were amped-up cop headlights—he moved like he was in strobe. He stopped in the lights and shook there, and when he took his next step, his feet went out from under him and he landed with a thud on his back.

"Wait here," said Belliveau. He got out of the cruiser and went to the old man, who was crumpled in a ball on his side.

It was obvious Belliveau didn't quite know how to approach the situation. He seemed the kind of cop comfortable breaking up pot parties or patrolling the ice rink during hockey games, drinking hot chocolate and nodding and smirking at the moms who had been in his high school class. He crouched down next to the old man and rested a hand on his crumpled trench coat. The old man was still shaking, but then he turned and with great force the old man yelled "FREEZE!" and I saw that it was not an old man at all; it was Ziegler.

Belliveau leapt back, but only seemed startled for a second; then I saw his face blazing in the headlights. His eyes were wide and his mouth was open and he went after Ziegler with his hands up like a linebacker. Ziegler sprung up and raced across the lot. Belliveau was after him. This was not much of a contest. Ziegler was a streak to the dumpsters, leaving Belliveau alone in the orange fluorescent lights, galloping, black uniform cast against the snowpack. I'll give it to Officer Friendly: he had a long stride and put in an admirable effort. He was just fat and slow.

At the dumpsters, again Belliveau was outmatched. We knew those dumpsters well. There was a crawl space underneath the middle one, and that's where Ziegler was hiding. I could see his breath coming out from below. Ziegler could have just sprinted over the snowbank again, but he wanted to mess with Belliveau, so just as Belliveau went looking behind the dumpsters, Ziegler shot out from the crawl space and was sprinting back across the lot. He was coming toward me, yelling, "Fuckface! Get out of the car!" Belliveau was still kicking like hell, and just as he sputtered a breathless "Freeze!" he belly-flopped on the snowpack.

Ziegler got to the cruiser and screamed, "Let's go!"

I pointed back in the direction of Belliveau. He was face-down, arms spread, legs spread, as though he had been dropped from the sky.

I got out of the cruiser and stood next to Ziegler and we stared back at Belliveau. He started moving his arms awkwardly, like he was trying to make a snow angel, but only in a lazy kind of way.

The first steps we took toward Belliveau felt wrong. Then we ran, and when we got to him, we could hear him moaning. Steam rose from his back. We struggled to flip him over. He had a scratch on his forehead, spit pooling on his chin, and two

slugs of snot coming from his nostrils. He said, "My pocket."
We just crouched there as he fumbled his hands around his
belly. His eyes were wide and his face was red. He almost
looked like a baby, jerking his arms without any real control. I
put my hand in the rough pocket of his patrol pants but didn't
find anything. Ziegler had his hand in the other pocket and he
took out a small tin. He handed it to Belliveau, but Belliveau
dropped it in the snow. Ziegler picked it up and handed it back
to Belliveau and Belliveau dropped it again. Then Ziegler
opened up the lid and took a tiny white pill from the tin and
placed it under Belliveau's raised tongue. Belliveau closed his
mouth, moaned again, held his chest, and rolled on his side.

"Let's get the fuck out of here," said Ziegler.

"Let's put him in the car," I said.

He could walk when the two of us flanked him, his arms
around our shoulders. He was still wheezing but seemed better. He didn't look at us. We laid him in the back of the cruiser.
Then Ziegler got in the driver's seat and picked up the part of
the radio you talk into, stretching the curled cord. "Officer
Friendly's hurt. He's at J.M. Biggies. We didn't do it."

He dropped the radio and we ran across the parking lot, past
the dumpsters, over the snowbank, and across the soccer field
behind the high school. The snow was over our knees so we
had to high-step. I thought Ziegler knew where he was going
and he probably thought I knew where I was going. There
were several fields linked up to the soccer field, most of them
overgrown with crinkled milkweeds sticking up through the
snow. We ran through a bunch of fields, too winded to talk. It
was actually a pretty nice night, cold with lots of moonlight and

no wind. I suspected we might be taking the fields in a round-about loop to Ziegler's brother's house. That was Wedge; he was a pothead who worked at Radio Shack and lived on his own. As we walked through the last field, I trudged in Ziegler's tracks, and when we got to Hanover Street we sat on a snow-bank to catch our breath. All the nearby houses were dark.

"Johnny fucking Anderson," I said.

"What about him?" said Ziegler.

"His mom married Officer Friendly."

"Shitty luck."

Ziegler kicked an ice ball into the street and watched breath steam from his mouth. Then he got up and I followed; we walked the two blocks to Wedge's house. We could see from the light in the windows that his TV was on. We bounded up the stairs and through the front door. His living room was aglow with the show he was watching and Wedge was stretched out in his La-Z-Boy with a canister of potato chips. We jumped on his couch.

"What's up, boys," said Wedge. It was his usual greeting.

We were still winded, and my face burned from the heat of the room. My feet were numb. Wedge ate his chips and laughed at the TV.

"Hey, Wedge," said Ziegler. "We're fucking heroes."

THE EDGE OF THE FOREST AND
THE EDGE OF THE OCEAN

HE'D BEEN KISSING MELANIE WASHINGTON MCCONNELL as he moved to the door, telling her with a smile he needed to get to work, that he couldn't be late, and in the mudroom, as he reached for the doorknob, she'd gotten on her knees amid all those boots and unbuckled his belt and he was immediately ready again, but he insisted he needed to go, that they both should get going—Melanie was a teacher at Point Allison Regional, too; she taught civics. They would be traveling in separate cars, of course, and they would drive different routes, too. They had, after all, been seen together often since she'd started that fall. Melanie stood up and hugged him, telling him she wanted him back that evening. Her husband was a cop who'd hit a stretch of night shifts, midnight to noon.

And when he came down the hollows in his Caprice—

blueberry fields on either side of the road, sunlit boulders and all those tiny light green leaves—he kept his foot firmly on the accelerator, and the car responded effortlessly, the warm vinyl bench seat floating on the chassis, the chassis floating on the road. It wasn't that Ian wasn't used to being happy—he remembered being happy—it was just that since he'd gotten out of the shower with Melanie, all the edges of everything were shining. He thought about his car's rubber tires on the dark, unblemished asphalt, how nice and quiet it all was, how satisfying the blue of the sky was; he cracked the window and smelled the wind coming off the ocean, warming, and he turned on his radio, WFUR's "Hot Sounds," and he tapped the top of the steering wheel along with the music (on a different day the self-consciousness of such an action would have embarrassed him)—it was a song he didn't recognize but one he immediately loved, couldn't get enough of—and by the end of the song he was screaming the chorus, *That was when it all came down, baby, that was when it all came down!* His hair was still wet from the shower; he could smell the shampoo and soap he'd used. It was seven-fifteen in the morning and he was heading to work. He was an English teacher at the junior high school; he had twenty-five seventh-graders in his homeroom and the first bell would be ringing at eight o'clock sharp.

Ian was not anxious about the consequences. Being with Melanie was worth the risk. Yes, there was the chance Melanie's husband Ack McConnell would find him out and hunt him down; this was true. But for now, in his warm car, he was singing. He was not worried about anything but getting through the day and returning to Melanie's house at the appointed hour—only slightly anxious that during the course of the day his penis would somehow be removed from his body so he wouldn't be able to visit her again, but otherwise, he was doing great. He felt like a man of purpose, of secret agendas.

The Point Skyler Bridge sat high above the bay, built into cliffs on either side of the Soper Island Narrows, 170 feet over the bay, and Ian looked left, clear up the Manganuk River, then right toward the open ocean, at the faint band of outer islands, Cuxabexis, Spencer, Musquacook. The water was a sheet of blue cloth; he had the strong feeling that if he were to swim at that moment he would be able to breathe below the surface; that he'd be quick as a seal; that the normally dark, cold water would be warm and well lit, like a hotel pool.

Also in view, there on the catwalk of the bridge, between two of the towering girders, was Alex Von Ballenberg—his best friend from high school—facing the bay.

Ian waved as he sped by Von Ballenberg, then started down the other side of the bridge. He remembered the night before graduation, over ten years earlier, when Ian and Von Ballenberg had left Kevin Goodale's party to walk the bridge. It was late May and cold, but they were warmed by the vodka in their stomachs, and at the crest of the bridge they stood on the catwalk together, looking for a while at the moonlight on the waves, before Von Ballenberg moved between two suspension cables and scampered down beneath the catwalk. Ian hated that Von Ballenberg had done this; it made him nervous, made him feel like a wimp, made him imagine what the *Courier-Gazette* would say if one of them fell, but after standing there alone for

a minute—there were no cars on the bridge, no sounds any-
where except for Von Ballenberg's whistling—Ian climbed
down the thin-runged steel ladder on the edge of the catwalk.
He saw that Von Ballenberg was gripping an I beam, dangling
over the black maw of the ocean.

"Oh, Jesus," Ian had said, but he collected himself, not
wanting to sound too serious. "Come on, man, come back to
the ladder."

Hand over hand, Von Ballenberg made his way toward Ian,
then grabbed the ladder.

"You try it," said Von Ballenberg.

"Okay, but just for a second," said Ian.

Facing the ladder, Ian reached out over his head, one
sweaty hand at a time, to grip the I beam. Then he let his legs
swing out over the bay. His fingers were strong against the cold
metal, and he could feel the wind blow against him. He looked
down at the crisp pattern of waves in the moonlight, feeling
pulled toward the ocean, as though he had weights in his pockets. "Scoot out a little further," said Von Ballenberg. "It feels
better out there." Ian scooted further. Von Ballenberg reached
out to grip the I beam, too. He hung facing Ian.

"Okay," said Ian. "Now my arms are tired."

Von Ballenberg shook his head, smiling.

"Come on, man," said Ian.

"Relax," said Von Ballenberg.

"Shit, stop this," said Ian.

Then Von Ballenberg got quiet, and Ian quieted down, too,
knowing the more he protested, the longer Von Ballenberg

would make him hang there. Ian's arms burned and his fingers stiffened.

After a few minutes, Von Ballenberg said, "Okay."

They climbed back up and sprinted down the catwalk, off the bridge, and back toward the woods. As they ran, the structures of the bridge seemed unimportant: all Ian really noticed was the sky. They were so high up, and he was running so fast, it felt like he was flying.

IAN KEPT HIS FOOT ON THE GAS, AND SOON THE ROAD WAS IN the woods again. The question of what Von Ballenberg was actually doing up there on the bridge so early in the morning came to him like an awkwardly rushed punch line to an unsuccessful joke, and this perplexed him greatly—how it had possibly seemed anything but unusual that Von Ballenberg was standing on the catwalk. Ian hadn't seen much of Von Ballenberg lately, but at first the only thought that had crossed his floating, zigzagging, sex-sated mind was a slight tinge of envy; he wished he could have been enjoying the day from Von Ballenberg's vantage point—it would have been a better place to spend the day than at Point Allison Regional Junior-Senior High; it would have been a nice place for Ian to contemplate the good fortune which had recently come his way. If he had been in Von Ballenberg's shoes, he would have squinted at the islands, remembering his job as ferry crew on the boat to Cuxabexis—his skinny body in that gas-station-attendant outfit the ferry captain made him wear—remembering it as the same summer he became obsessed with Melanie. Then he would have thought again about the warm slippery glory of being in the shower with her just minutes earlier.

He'd called her for the first time the spring of their junior year of high school. Ian drove to school then—in fact, he drove Von Ballenberg, too—and every day they would pass Melanie at her bus stop on West Elm, where she'd be sitting in the grass, or, if it was winter, standing with her arms folded, wearing a black stocking cap. Ian would often ask for Von Ballenberg's advice, wondering if they should just stop like the bus would stop and pick her up, drive her to school, and Von Ballenberg would say, Yes, absolutely, do it, come on, do it, but the idea made Ian clutch; there was no way he could try such a thing.

One morning that spring they were driving to school when Von Ballenberg bent down, looking for something under the seat. They were approaching Melanie's bus stop, and when Von Ballenberg was hidden from view, he reached past Ian's right knee to honk the horn. Melanie raised her head and looked flatly at Ian. Ian had no choice but to wave, which Melanie matched with a confused, gentle lifting of her own hand from her lap, not quite a wave, but a reluctant acknowledgment. In the next few days he thought about her endlessly, and he thought about calling her. And thought and thought. The details of her face shimmered in his mind: her dark eyebrows and blond hair and serious mouth, serious eyes. He rehearsed the conversation to himself.

Hello, Melanie?

or Hello, Melanie Washington?

or Hello, is this Melanie? Melanie Washington? Hi, it's Ian Merrick. You don't know me.

or You don't know me, but I have a funny story. You remember that time when that kid you didn't know drove by your bus stop, and he honked and waved? Well, that was me, only I wasn't the one who honked! It was my friend Alex Von Ballenberg. What a card.

or Hey, are your legs tired? They must be, because you've been running through my mind all day.

or Melanie, it's Ian, and it's actually not that important that you don't know who I am, because we're just two lonely souls marching around on earth, trapped in our bodies like sausages in their casings, but not like sausages because we're not actually connected to one another . . . that comparison doesn't quite work . . . but anyway, I was just wondering . . . would you like to go to the movies?

When he did call her, it had gone like this: he didn't respond when she said hello. She said it again, "Hello?" but again he stayed quiet.

Then, "Hi. Sorry. Um, Melanie Washington? Hi. It's Ian Merrick. I'm in your grade at school. In your Spanish class, actually."

"Juan?" she asked.

"What?"

"Isn't that what Señor Flaherty calls you? Juan?"

"No, I'm José," he said. "And I . . . lost the assignment. Or, I guess, I didn't write it down. Do you have it?"

"Oh, sure. Just a minute. Let me check."

There was a bumping sound, and the clapping of books on a desk, and other sounds, *the sounds of Melanie in her house, moving around*, and he was cold with nervousness, his heart beating and his white hands clutching the phone—the earpiece fused to his head—then she was on again, "Yup, here it is. We just have to learn those verbs on page 290. That's all."

"Okay," he said, breathing again. "Thanks a lot. I hope I'm not calling at a bad time."

"No way, José," she said.

"What?"

"Just a joke. No way, José. You know?"

"Oh. Ha!" he said, all wrong. "That's . . . a good one. Okay, bye."

"Bye," she said.

"See ya."

"Bye."

When Ian thought about his former self, his high school self, he got shivers, wondering if, possibly, it all hadn't been as bad as he remembered. There'd been some good times, right? He hadn't always been a total spineless wretch, right? Well, unfortunately, he had been. Almost always. There was one slight reprieve, during that summer working on the ferry to Cuxabexis when he wore the gas-station garb and worked with men who were all at least ten years older than he was; his job was to park cars and load propane tanks, and sometimes the passengers chatted him up—the summer people coming up from Boston and New York—they didn't know he was a terrified high school kid, they just thought he was authentic. One perfect Friday there'd been this older girl from Connecticut who had been fascinated by him; they sat on the side rail by the wheelhouse as they steamed to the island and she asked him questions, rapid fire, about the boat and cormorants and fisheries and red tide and winter weather, and despite his usual terror, and despite the way the sun hit her neck, making her skin look unusually touchable, he spoke to her more frankly and confidently than he'd ever spoken to any girl before—he knew he'd be spending only an hour of his life with her, and that he'd never see her again, and so he made up answers to the questions she asked. The assurance she gave him, by just finding him interesting, had allowed him to call Melanie again.

IAN PULLED OVER TO THE GRAVEL SHOULDER, THEN CRANKED the wheel, U-turned, and drove back toward the bridge. He looked at his hands on the wheel, and at his watch: it was seven-thirty; there was still plenty of time to make the first bell. He liked to get there early, though, so he could sit at his desk for a few minutes before the students were in their seats, glumly staring at him. He would double-check the marked passages from *Julius Caesar* he planned to read aloud. Then, as usual, he'd close his eyes and think of absolutely nothing, knowing, in truth, that the better prepared he was, the worse he'd perform in class; the fear of not knowing what to say ahead of time forced him to actually think.

Ian parked the Caprice on the shoulder near the edge of the cliffs, under the spruce trees. He jogged on the walkway toward the peak of the bridge, listening to the wind whistle around the towers, watching his feet as he ran, not wanting to trip, not wanting to look over the edge.

When Ian and Von Ballenberg had lived next door to each

other and been best friends, Von Ballenberg had loathed Ian's Brittany spaniel, Chelsea—whom Ian loved very much—and the basis of Von Ballenberg's hatred of Chelsea was that he claimed she took shits on the Von Ballenberg lawn in the dead of night, that the dog was the only dog Von Ballenberg knew who was too ashamed to poop in broad daylight. It was not the shits themselves, Von Ballenberg claimed, it was the dog's shame which repulsed him, the stealth shitting. Ian went to great lengths to defend his dog—he loved her, loved even her modesty. He tried to cover for her, lying on her behalf. But the evidence was stacked against Chelsea: Ian's family had a dog door off the kitchen, which allowed her passage to and from the house at any hour, and there were no shits on the Merrick family lawn, only on the Von Ballenberg's.

To gather evidence Von Ballenberg stayed up one night—all night—staked behind the hedge in front of his house, adjacent to the lawn. What Von Ballenberg captured on film—with a high-powered flash—was not Chelsea in that distinctive hunch, neck extended, back haunches strained—but Ian himself coming out onto the Von Ballenberg lawn, dropping his pants and squatting for the camera. It was a joke—at the time Ian thought it was masterfully funny—but the next week at school the photo was posted in at least three prominent places, including the double doors leading into the cafeteria. The film had captured Ian in profile, his features in plain view (he was smiling), the blinding whiteness of his upper thighs exposed to the world.

And the stress of girls . . . Von Ballenberg was a reckless charmer, a fact which Ian couldn't dispute, but which tormented him, because not only was Von Ballenberg attractive—

with his broad shoulders, smooth skin, and thick black hair—but he also knew how to play the crowd. Knew how to keep his stock price up. The girls at school loved Von Ballenberg. There'd been a day in the fall of their junior year, when Ian was walking quietly down the school's main hallway, heading to orchestra rehearsal, when he saw Von Ballenberg with Kate Bishop, a shy, honest girl with long braided brown hair. The hallway had ceilings which rose high above the lockers, and multipaned windows facing the soccer field. Von Ballenberg's back was to Ian, but he could see Kate—her red cheeks, her slight smile, and her eyes. It was her eyes which exposed her. She looked close to crying, but Ian recognized this not as sadness, but as urgency. Kate Bishop had been Ian's Chemistry lab partner—she was meticulous and diligent and intensely private—but here she was, laid bare. Ian wanted to shout to her: It's just Von Ballenberg! He waited up all night in a hedge, hoping to take pictures of a shitting dog! Instead Ian turned around. He skipped rehearsal.

Ian called Melanie again but only about their Spanish assignments, and in the fall Von Ballenberg blew up at Ian as they were driving to school. He said he didn't know what Ian saw in Melanie; she was such a freak, the way she wore that black stocking cap and never smiled. "You're going to waste all your time on her. All you do is think about her and you don't do anything about it, and one day she's going to take you behind the school and suck your blood, or cut you up into little bits."

"Fuck yourself," said Ian.

"I swear she's in a cult," said Von Ballenberg.

"Maybe you're jealous," said Ian.

"Now that's a good one," said Von Ballenberg. "How could I possibly be jealous of a faggot like you?"

Ian pulled over; they were in front of Stegger's package store on Main Street, just two blocks from the elementary school. A crossing guard was ushering a pack of bundled-up kids across the street.

"Out," said Ian.

"No," he said.

"You're walking. I'm not driving you anymore."

"I'm not getting out," said Von Ballenberg. Ian couldn't push things further; Von Ballenberg was simply bigger and stronger than Ian was, and Ian didn't want to be late to school. They didn't speak of it again, though what Ian wanted more than anything was to win over Melanie—to get her to notice him—so that he could prove to Von Ballenberg that he had guts.

But instead Ian immersed himself in the details of Von Ballenberg's sex life—it was easier than calling Melanie again. He asked Von Ballenberg to describe every moment of every one of his exploits. For this they would go to Von Ballenberg's bedroom, overlooking the lawn where Chelsea (perhaps) shat in the dead of night; Von Ballenberg would close and lock the door, and he would be happy to oblige. There in the bedroom would be Ian and Von Ballenberg and the imaginary girl; Von Ballenberg would mime the first move—taking her hand while they walked through the cemetery, or giving her a back rub beside the soccer field ("Now, when I give a back rub," said Von Ballenberg, "I don't just rub the shoulders; I rub the arms, too, and the elbows and forearms and hands and fingers")—and then, invariably, instantaneously, Von Ballenberg would have the imaginary girl on her back. In a snap, their clothes would be off. During these performances for Ian—lifting imaginary legs, donning an imaginary condom—Von Ballenberg would grin, consumed by the reenactment, not gloating, really, but not concerned, either, by how all of it might be received by Ian, who hadn't yet kissed a girl. After all, Ian had wanted to know. He had wanted details, and Von Ballenberg was delivering them up, generously.

These sessions became less painful and less frequent when Von Ballenberg seemed to settle for a while on Samantha Sheppard, the daughter of the rink manager, Buddy Sheppard. At first Von Ballenberg was still interested in describing to Ian all of the lines they crossed in their movement toward what Von Ballenberg called "CSM" (Complete Sexual Mastery), but eventually the reenactments bored Von Ballenberg, and they just made Ian sad. This was around the time they graduated from Point Allison Junior-Senior High. Samantha got pregnant that summer, and for a few weeks Von Ballenberg seemed angry with Ian. She wanted to keep the baby, and Von Ballenberg didn't, and while Von Ballenberg hadn't asked Ian for his opinion, he knew what Ian would say.

At the end of a hot, rainy day in late August, they were out behind the school, on the soccer field, a place where they could talk without being heard. The field was soaked; it smelled like alewives and clay—like the river.

"Why is this happening?" Von Ballenberg yelled. "This can't be happening."

"It's happening," said Ian.

"Why?" he yelled again.

"Well . . . " said Ian.

"What do you mean, 'well'?"

"You've kind of had this coming, haven't you?"

Von Ballenberg shoved him down. As Von Ballenberg walked away, Ian stayed sitting on the field, looking up at the clearing sky, letting the water soak through his clothes.

Von Ballenberg and Samantha moved into Anchors Away, an apartment complex on the Royal River. Ian didn't speak to Von Ballenberg again until he attended their wedding that fall, at the Sheppards' house on Sligo Road, where Buddy built a dance floor in the milkweed field out back. They had a DJ, and wine and kegs of beer, and two bonfires. Late in the evening, Von Ballenberg approached Ian on the dance floor, gave him a hug, and called him his best friend. They walked out into the milkweed.

"She miscarried," said Von Ballenberg.

"I'm sorry," said Ian, but he knew Von Ballenberg was relieved.

That winter Ian and Von Ballenberg got together every Tuesday night to drink at the Somesville Grill, where they'd play darts or watch hockey. Ian was a full-time student at Orono, but he drove the three hours to Point Allison every Tuesday afternoon. Von Ballenberg worked as a prep cook at Mary's Restaurant, on Hanover Street in Point Allison, and kept Tuesday nights free. At the bar, Von Ballenberg never said a word about Samantha, and Ian never asked. The next summer Ian lived in Vermont, where he worked at a private school teaching summer classes, and the following year he came back to Point Allison only rarely. He heard from a classmate that Von Ballenberg and Samantha had split.

HE APPROACHED HIS OLD FRIEND AT THE CREST OF THE bridge, where bright sunlight paled the copper green girders. The wind was blowing at his back, so in profile his shoulder-length black hair hid his face. His trenchcoat was open like a cape. The catwalk was the edge of the bridge, built not for pedestrians but for maintenance purposes; the suspension cables were attached near the edge, too, but there was nothing else keeping those on the catwalk from stepping out into the sky.

"What are you doing?" asked Ian.

"Oh, just thinking, really. I always liked it up here," said Von Ballenberg, grabbing a suspension cable and leaning his body out over the water, curling the toe of one of his shoes over the edge of the catwalk. Von Ballenberg's face was washed out and thin. Ian was surprised that seeing Von Ballenberg made him want to be in high school again—he rarely had good feelings about that time in his life—but now he wanted everything to matter less again, he wanted the car pool, and another shot at defending his dog.

"No work today?" asked Ian. He didn't even know what Von Ballenberg was doing for a job—he'd owned a restaurant in Somesville at one point, but that had been a few years ago.

"Nope—today it's just me and the sky, me and the bridge."

Ian looked at the islands in the distance. They seemed closer than usual; there was no humidity in the air; the sky, even at the horizon, was clear blue. "Sorry to hear about you and Samantha," he said.

"Fuck it. It was bound to happen."

Ian looked down and felt his stomach rise, his feet numb, but the water made him stare—it was dark purple, the wind whitening the swells. He saw the water every day; it always got him staring. He imagined the free fall and it made him sick to his stomach. The wind swirled around them, shifting often, little gusts from all sides. It was a long way down: Ian could see the miniature swells crashing onshore but he couldn't hear them.

Ian himself had thought about suicide in the past—not that he'd actually ever do it (he knew he wouldn't) or that his life was ever that bad—but he was fascinated by the idea. The resolve it would require. The balls. On the bridge, it was there for the taking: that first step into the air.

"So . . . Von Ballenberg," said Ian. "I just want to tell you, I really don't think this is a good idea, being up here."

"Christ," said Von Ballenberg.

"I just . . . well, what are you doing here?"

Von Ballenberg squinted at him.

"You won't do anything stupid, will you?" asked Ian.

"You mean, jump?" said Von Ballenberg, and with the fingers of his right hand he mimed walking to the edge, leaping, falling.

"Well, yeah," said Ian.

Von Ballenberg laughed. "Stupid? I think if I jumped off

here I'd be a little more than stupid. I'd be kaput."

Ian saw an approaching car slow down, and he turned toward it; it was Principal Andrews, Ian's boss, with his white hair and both hands on the wheel. He looked quizzically at Ian. Then he yelled, "You okay out there, son?"

"Yes sir, we're fine. Just taking a look at the view," he said.

"You sure you're okay?" Honking cars were backed up behind him.

Ian nodded and waved. Principal Andrews waved and pulled away. Ian felt the urge to sprint back to his car and try to beat the old man to school, to show him that everything was perfectly normal, but instead he turned back to Von Ballenberg, then glanced at his watch. It was seven forty-five.

"You have a plan, here?" asked Ian.

"No plan," said Von Ballenberg.

"Come on. Let's go."

"You don't believe me," said Von Ballenberg. "You think I'm here to jump, don't you."

"No, I believe you," Ian lied. "So let's get out of here. Or, at least, I should probably get going."

He looked at his watch, too. "Yeah, I've got to go as well," said Von Ballenberg.

"Okay, come on," said Ian.

"Right," said Von Ballenberg. He rubbed his hands together, tucked his hair behind his ears, and spread his arms like a diver on the high board. Ian grabbed him by the back of his coat.

"Jesus," said Ian.

"Shit, you're an angel! What would I ever do without you?"

said Von Ballenberg, laughing. "You're a stitch, Ian. You really are."

It was at this time normally that Ian would be tapping his black shoes up the marble steps of Point Allison Junior-Senior High School's front entrance, not making eye contact with the students milling by the Golden Trojan statue mounted near the double doors; the kids there wore angry looks and their lips were pierced with metal hoops; they were scrawny, pale, pirate-like kids wearing pants and hooded sweatshirts three sizes too big, all of them playing it cool but curiously attracted to the seven-foot Golden Trojan, with its fantastic posture and wide, shiny chest—their mother ship. Ian knew these kids; none of them were in his classes but he knew them. They were the terrified. It was eight o'clock now and he missed them.

"I need to make a call," said Ian, reaching into the pocket of his blazer for his phone. He dialed the school. The principal's secretary answered. "Could you please page Mrs. McConnell for me?" he asked.

"McConnell?" said Von Ballenberg.

Ian covered the phone, looking up. "Will you shut up please?"

"She's your girlfriend?"

"She's my colleague."

Von Ballenberg grinned and clapped his hands. "You're fucking her."

Ian wanted to be the kind of person who could keep a straight face under fire, but he couldn't. He looked down and smiled.

"I'm with you," said Von Ballenberg. "I know that ground, buddy."

"It's all pretty new," said Ian.

"I mean, I know that ground, specifically. Melanie. Your old obsession. She's married to that cop, Ack McConnell. I know the whole story. We used to have a thing."

Melanie picked up the phone. "Hello?"

"*What?*" said Ian.

"Ian?" she asked.

Ian covered the phone and looked at Von Ballenberg. "*What?*" he whispered, loudly.

"We had a thing for a little while," said Von Ballenberg. "A little thing. For a little while."

"Hello?" asked Melanie.

Ian uncovered the phone. "Melanie," he said, quietly. "I'm sorry. Could you check up on my homeroom? I'm running behind."

"Hi, Mrs. McConnell!" yelled Von Ballenberg.

"Who's that?" asked Melanie.

"That's somebody else," said Ian. "We're sorting something out. I'll be there soon."

"Where are you?" she asked.

"I'm on the bridge," he said. "It's a long story."

"Are you okay?"

"Great. Okay. Yes."

"What's going on, Ian?" she asked.

"I've got to go. But thanks for checking my kids for me. See you soon." He closed the phone. "Tell me, now," he said.

"It was when you were freaking out about her. When you couldn't pull yourself together. I never told you?"

"No, you never told me," said Ian.

"I wanted to check things out. For your benefit, of course."

"Are you serious?" Ian yelled.

"No," he said, smiling and shaking his head. "God, you are still so easy."

"Oh, for Christ's sake," said Ian. "You bastard."

"I just wanted to test how much you like her," he said.

It was disorienting: to feel as though he had his act together more than Von Ballenberg did. He didn't want to pity Von Ballenberg—Ian had been down on his luck before, too—but the whole business of putting up with Von Ballenberg's crap on the bridge at eight in the morning—it was absurd. Ian was an adult and late for work. Ian knew his life in the past few years had been motoring along fine without Von Ballenberg. He knew that what he probably should have done when he first saw Von Ballenberg on the bridge was to keep driving. But this was a delicate situation; he still didn't know, for sure, why Von Ballenberg was standing near the edge. He didn't want to leave him there, head to school, then find out later his old friend had killed himself.

"Give me your wallet," said Ian. He'd read of this strategy somewhere—the best way to deal with someone in Von Ballenberg's condition was to make casual references to death.

Von Ballenberg looked at him.

"You've got your wallet on you, don't you?"

"What?" said Von Ballenberg.

"And your watch. That's got to be worth something. You're going to die anyway, and I've got to get to school."

Von Ballenberg stared at Ian; his eyes weren't fixed on Ian's eyes, they were looking at a point lower down, at his mouth, or his chin. "That's a damn good idea," said Von Ballenberg. He stepped away from the edge and removed his long rectangular brown leather wallet from the back pocket of his corduroys. He handed it to Ian. Then he unclasped his watchband and slipped the chunky gold-colored thing off his wrist, and handed it over. Von Ballenberg's reaction to Ian's request was surprising, but at least now he had his answer. The strategy had backfired, but at least he knew what he was dealing with.

"Ian," said Von Ballenberg, quietly.

"You don't have to apologize," said Ian, as compassionately as possible.

"For fuck's sake," yelled Von Ballenberg. He grabbed Ian by the front of his shirt and pulled him close. "I ought to throw *you* off the bridge. Listen to me, Merrick," he yelled. "I'm not jumping. You got that? I'm just up here hanging out. Having a goddamn moment." He shook Ian and Ian dropped the watch and the wallet. The wallet landed with a slap against the wooden catwalk, but the watch fell between the two slats.

"Oh," said Ian.

Von Ballenberg got on his hands and knees to look through the crack. "There it goes," he said. "Four hundred dollars." He picked up the wallet and put it back in his pocket.

Ian got on his hands and knees, too, and looked for the falling watch. "That's a long way down," he said.

"You're absolutely crazy," said Von Ballenberg.

"Man, I'm sorry," he said. "I just didn't want you to do anything stupid."

"You know, I think I can hold it together without you, shit for brains."

Ian looked at Von Ballenberg's pale face, his thin nose and dark eyes; the anger and embarrassment Ian felt was familiar, but he hadn't felt it in a long time.

"That whole, 'Give me your wallet' routine—wow, that's a fantastic approach," said Von Ballenberg. "You're a real pro, Ian."

Traffic was picking up. It was just after eight, and Ian could see that someone was running out the walkway from the east side of the bridge, where Ian's Caprice was parked.

"Someone's coming," said Ian.

"Perfect," said Von Ballenberg, sighing. "Another Good Samaritan." He stepped back from the edge and folded his arms on his chest.

It was Melanie, wearing a blue skirt and white blouse and no shoes. Ten yards away, she stopped running. Her chin and her cheeks were red; her hair was still wet; she looked beautiful and strong in her school clothes, but she looked less like a teacher than someone dressed up as one.

"Hi," Ian and Von Ballenberg said together.

"You guys okay?" she asked.

"I'm okay," said Von Ballenberg. "This guy's a little whacked, but I'm fine."

Ian took a few steps toward her and said, quietly, "Melanie, I think I can handle this. Don't worry; we're okay."

"This? Handle this? If anyone's nuts, if anyone's liable to jump off this bridge, it's him," said Von Ballenberg, pointing at Ian.

"No one's nuts," said Ian.

"I'm certainly not nuts," said Von Ballenberg.

"I don't think we've ever actually met," said Melanie. "But you're Alex Von Ballenberg, right?"

"Yes, ma'am," said Von Ballenberg, nodding. It was moments like these, Ian knew, when his old friend had always been most comfortable. "And you're Melanie."

"You know, girls used to be crazy about you, back then. Like you were Elvis or something," she said. She said "back then" as though it were eons ago, and Ian liked this.

"It was fun being Elvis," said Von Ballenberg.

"I suppose it would have been," she said, smiling half-heartedly.

She moved her gaze to the bay. "I've always wondered what it would look like, standing here," said Melanie. "Is that Spencer, there?" She pointed at the outer islands. "That whale-shaped one?"

"That's Cuxabexis," said Ian. He could see the speck of the ferry, silent, its wake a thin white tail. He couldn't believe it, really, that the three of them were having a conversation; sometimes it seemed as though nothing ever changed, but at that moment, he felt continents shifting in his mind. Melanie had come to the bridge because she'd been worried by his phone call, and Von Ballenberg was no longer Elvis.

"When did you move back?" asked Von Ballenberg.

"This fall," she said.

"My condolences," said Von Ballenberg.

"I'm glad to be back, actually," she said.

"Huh," said Von Ballenberg, shaking his head. "So . . . you guys are an item now?"

"Jesus," said Ian.

"Well, I'm married, actually," said Melanie.

"That's what I heard," said Von Ballenberg. "But sounds like you guys are getting some on the side, too."

Ian put his hands up. "I didn't tell him."

"Well, it's the truth," said Melanie. "I suppose I've got to get used to it. Things with Ack are pretty much over."

"Which is not to say he isn't going to kill you, Ian," said Von Ballenberg.

Melanie cocked her head gently to the side and rubbed the back of her neck, squinting. Ian had seen the gesture on a few occasions since he'd started spending time with her. It meant, roughly, Okay, now what? He loved this about her, that she was practical. In the fall, when he first laid eyes on her again after so many years, he nearly collapsed. He was walking down the main hallway, passing classrooms, and he saw her in one of them, at the chalkboard—she had a loud, clear voice; her students were quiet; he stood there trying to believe it was her. He listened to her until she turned toward him—they caught eyes and he lurched out of view. It took them four months to become friends, because he didn't want to let on he'd been thinking about her for ten years—their conversations in the faculty lounge were always oddly formal. He felt he needed to treat her like a stranger. But after she asked him to eat with her at the Miss Somesville Diner one night, they had dinner there together any chance they could. (Ack rarely crossed the Point Allison town line, as a cop or otherwise.)

And Ian first kissed her just the night before, when the diner was empty and their waitress was in the kitchen. They were sitting across from each other in a booth. During a stretch of silence, Melanie turned to look out the window, and Ian leaned over and kissed her quickly on the cheek, dryly. She didn't move. He sat back. When she turned toward him again, she didn't mention the kiss directly, but they were on auto-pilot, then. They talked for two more hours, long after the sounds of silverware and plates from the back had faded. After midnight, they drove to her house.

The Cuxabexis ferry was entering the mouth of Point Allison harbor; from the bridge, Ian could tell the captain had already throttled down the engine—its wake was hard to see. Sometimes, he could recognize the town for what it was, as he did then: a few houses and boats on the edge of the forest and the edge of the ocean.

He hadn't even known her in high school, and yet he'd hung on to dreams of her. And there were so many things, destructive things, that his mind made him believe: that he'd never find love, that he'd never figure out what he was doing wrong.

A siren screamed in the distance, and as soon as they all turned toward the sound they saw the faint blue warbling lights coming down into the hollow, heading toward the bridge.

"Oh, crap," said Melanie. "That's my husband."

"I guess it's time to break up this party," said Von Ballenberg.

Melanie grabbed Ian's hand and they ran on the catwalk, toward the Caprice, away from the siren. Von Ballenberg followed them.

But Ian pulled back on Melanie's hand, and she turned toward him, expectantly. They stopped, and Von Ballenberg stopped behind them.

"Maybe we shouldn't run," said Ian.

"You should run," said Von Ballenberg.

"Ack doesn't take to reason very well," said Melanie.

"Okay, next time. Next time I won't run. I want things to work out for us, Melanie," he said.

She squeezed his hand. "Let's get going," she said.

Von Ballenberg, for the moment, stayed quiet. When they started running again, all he said was, "Why am I running with you fools?" but Ian knew why. It felt great to run on the catwalk, when you were so high up, looking out at the sky—it felt like you were flying.

THE TOAST

I TOOK THE WEEKEND OFF FROM MY JOB TENDING BAR AT the Waterfront Grill in Portland and drove to Point Allison, where my mother was summering with a guy named Hutch whom she had married earlier that year. They'd been asking me to visit for months. When I arrived, Mom was in the garden, stooped over a ball of rhododendron roots she was trying to fit in a hole. Her hair was longer and lighter than it had been. Hutch was shirtless, reclining in a wicker settee on the porch, wearing aviator glasses and reading a paperback. The things my mother had bragged about him over the phone were that he was an adman—he'd made a name for himself by using homely actors to sell makeup—and that he still found a way to spend three months in Maine during the summer; despite his wealth, he mowed the lawn every Saturday, if it wasn't raining. Also, she said his mother used to write a syndicated column for the *Globe* and his father had been a United States congressman from the area north of Boston. The wedding, Mom went on to say, had been a gas; his family owned the entire peninsula and it had been a three-day free-for-all. There'd been politicians eating psilocybic toadstools and renowned journalists swimming in the ocean in all their clothes. There had been lots of sexual energy, she said, and a swing orchestra played under a tent on back-to-back nights.

When she came out to my car, Hutch followed her, putting his sunglasses up in his thick gray hair. She kissed me on the cheek and squeezed me at the waist for a long time. Afterwards, Hutch gave me a tight handshake.

"Look at this guy. He's fit as a fiddle," Hutch said in the deep voice of a stadium announcer. In fact, I felt entirely unfit, especially next to Hutch, a real varsity specimen. He had smooth freckled skin and large teeth, and while he was going soft in some areas, he retained the important muscles, the ones in his shoulders and his jaw. Mom, as usual, had come out ahead. My bet was that she would eventually tire of him, but for now, Hutch was handsome and he'd take her to good parties, which to Mom was essential.

The house was large, but even more impressive was the emerald field leading down to the ocean; most likely it had been cleared many generations back—it had no brambles or stumps like the newer fields in Maine. I was sure that before long Mom would be entertaining in the field; she'd get bonfires going and perhaps an elaborate version of Capture the Flag, with cocktails. Mom winked at me, which meant we would be nice to Hutch.

Then she put her hand on my cheek and said, "Your room's all ready, sweetie. There's a shower up there. Go on and relax." Hutch led me to my room on the second floor, which had a simple twin bed, painted pine floors, a rocking chair in the corner, and three small windows looking out at the field—and farther, at the islands in the bay.

I took off my shoes and socks, rolled up the cuffs of my jeans, and walked downstairs to the liquor cabinet, predictably located in the dining room. I poured myself some rum and found grapefruit juice in the chrome restaurant-style refrigerator in the kitchen. I walked into the living room, sat in a leather armchair next to a lamp made from the leg of a zebra. The sun on the ocean looked warm but the chair retained a coolness and I felt perfectly at ease in this stranger's house. The sea air and the brightness of the house made me feel limber and articulate. I dozed.

Mom woke me an hour later and told me there was time to shower and dress before we walked to the Wendells'. "Sweetie?" she asked.

"Yeah, Mom?" I rubbed my face.

"I want you to know how glad I am you've come to visit me," she said.

"Sure thing, Mom."

"Being here is different from anything we've had before. It's a whole new arena," she said. "It might take a while to get used to."

"I can imagine, Mom."

"Sweetie, these people will expect things of you," she said. "Just remember, you have everything they want."

"Sure I do, Mom," I said.

"It's Old Man Wendell's birthday. That's the occasion. He's Hutch's uncle," she said. "He's quite something—served three terms as governor of Maine." When she stood up, she kissed me on the top of my head and said, "These people will find out how great you are, I know it."

I went up to shower. Mom had given me similar pep talks all my life, beginning when I was very little, after Dad left and it was just the two of us. "You and I are the best people in the world," she'd say. "We're stronger and smarter than everyone. There isn't anything we can't do. That's our secret. We can't tell anyone our secret, because it will make them feel bad about themselves."

Later, when I was a teenager, she used a more serious tone. "It's our irresponsibility that gets us into trouble," she'd said. "It will follow us all our lives. Your grandfather was the first of our kind, the first swamp Yankee. His mind was crackerjack, but he drank himself to death. He killed himself because he was too excited. You and me . . . we're that excited, too."

The water pressure was urgent, the porcelain tiles had a muted sheen, the fixtures were solid and the plumbing was tight; it was a nice house in Maine. I stepped out with a red chest and combed a clear part in my hair. I still looked somewhat haggard around the eyes, but the shower had improved me. I put on a clean pair of jeans without underwear and a peach-colored shirt. I wore flip-flops. I didn't know what the people at the party would be wearing, but I would trump them with confidence. Hutch came into my room as I was getting ready to go downstairs.

"Roger, I wanted a minute with you, old boy, if it's okay," he said. He was barefoot in cotton pants and a white silk shirt. He had combed his gray hair straight back.

"Shoot," I said, sitting down on the bed.

"Your mother and I are glad you're here, buddy. Great to have you," he said, sitting down and clasping his hands together in his lap.

"I'm all for it," I said, smiling back at him.

"You'll find out the more time you spend here . . . it's a wonderful, wonderful spot," he said. Then his face turned serious. "But what you should know is that the people up here are very . . . um, close. They're going to love you, they're going to love you a lot. But it can be somewhat fierce."

"Sounds like my kind of folks," I said.

"I just want to sort of . . . brief you on the situation," he said. "Remember, though, it all comes from love."

"I'm all about love," I said. Hutch walked downstairs and I realized I disliked him. He and Mom waited on the front porch while I made myself another rum and drank it down.

We walked on a path through the woods to the Wendells'. It smelled of spruce and that soupy, stringy dirt under moss. Hutch was surefooted in the woods, holding Mom by the hand and pointing out roots to step over. I was beginning to see that the summer people of Point Allison didn't play golf for recreation; they chopped down trees with axes, sailed through storms, and had, I'm sure, on occasion spent nights sleeping on barren reefs or on bell buoys. He stopped to let me catch up and said, "Roger, you see how dense these woods are? It's old growth. My great-grandfather walked through here as a boy." The trail was deep, with flat pine needles and through the thicket you couldn't see the ocean, only small bits of sky. The dark shade made everything still. "None of these smaller trees or that moss down there would survive without the fog off the ocean blowing through. I've never seen any other woods like these."

He raised his eyebrows for emphasis. Mom and I listened, but I knew no man could really impress her.

"Ha," Mom said.

"Oh?" said Hutch.

"You should see the woods where Roger and I are from," Mom said. "Now they're unique. It's a moose thoroughfare. You see raw antler velvet on the trees, where they've been scratching, and big shits right in the trail. Their scent is everywhere."

"Sounds unpleasant," Hutch said. I had no idea which woods Mom was speaking of.

"Roger, you've got to watch these people and their rhetoric," she said, squeezing Hutch. "They think they're right all the time—and most of the time they are. But once in a while, you catch them exaggerating, you catch them in a wild exaggeration. It's some kind of Point Allison thing."

"Let me spin that if I may," he said. "What it is up here is enthusiasm. We are enthusiastic people. I won't deny that."

"Well, all right then," Mom said, rubbing his shoulder.

They kissed and the discussion ended.

The path opened up to a circular driveway paved with small pieces of white granite and the house, twenty yards from the high-tide mark, was surrounded by bay and rose bushes. It had a wraparound porch and a garage with an old matte green Cadillac. People waved at us from the porch.

We climbed the steps and Hutch turned back to me and said, "Here we go, old boy. Steel yourself."

I saw the crowd and thought myself wrongly dressed. A good portion of the guests were wearing costumes—plenty of flapper getups and Renaissance-era ruffled shirts—but thankfully people were already drinking heavily, their voices raised. The host rushed over wearing an Indian feathered headdress, kissing my mother on the lips before Hutch introduced us.

"Roger, this is my uncle, Hubie Wendell. You can call him the old man," he said. Like Hutch, the old man was handsome and strong. He wore leather chaps. His bare chest was broad and his forearms were tan and he was my height, even with his slight stoop.

"Welcome to the family," he boomed. His handshake was tighter than Hutch's, and he held it, and pumped it, and opened his eyes wide like a silent film star. "So glad to have you." He shook his head—and the headdress—up and down. "Plenty of attractive ladies at this party, my friend," he said, finally letting go. Like Hutch, he was barefoot, and I noticed that he stationed his toes with space between them and, leaning forward, flexed the knuckles. I thanked him for having me, slipped off my flip-flops, and stowed them under a deck chair; then I went to the bar.

I planned on sticking with rum, but the girl tending bar wasn't wearing a bra, so I seized up.

"Gin and tonic, please," I said. This was the calmer option.

The blue of the ocean and the smell of raw oysters was boiling me a bit. Gin would help. The bartender didn't move, she just squinted at me with a look of boredom and anger. Her eyes were huge and brown and she kept a deep, judgmental stare. I couldn't imagine anyone more beautiful. Her seriousness made me sweat. She maintained this face and didn't blink her eyes. She pushed her lips tightly together. This made my arms tingle and gave me a flash of self-awareness, but I forged ahead, pressing my toes against the deck boards. "Would a martini be better?" I asked. "How about a martini."

"Well, how are *you*?" she asked stiffly.

"I'm well," I said. "In need of a drink."

"I saw you come in," she snipped, reaching around behind her and grabbing two bottles of gin. She slammed them on the bar. "You didn't even look at me. Where have you been?"

"I've—been—" I started.

She leaned over and whispered, firmly. "It's been a long time and I haven't heard from you at all."

I took a quick glance behind me and said nothing.

"Just a letter, or a quick phone call. That's all I needed," she said.

I squinted back at her. Her eyes were rich brown and the pale spot where her collarbone met her neck was picking up the orange color of the tablecloth. I was almost willing to forget everything I had ever known and assume the identity of the person she thought I was. "Actually, maybe I don't need a drink," I said. "A glass of water would be fine, if it's not too much trouble."

"I need to see you," she said. "You need to meet me under the porch in five minutes."

She began to mix my drink. She gripped the Tanqueray, and the flashing motion of her smooth white arm made me seize up again. I was pleased she imagined herself in love with me. The Tanqueray was flooding my glass; she filled it to within an inch of the top, then overflowed the glass with tonic. She used a large knife—machete-like—to cut the lime slice, which she gently tapped onto the rim of the drink, then guided the whole mess to my hand.

"Goddamn it, I've missed you," she said. "And I need you. Five minutes." She raised one hand and outstretched the fingers.

I looked for a seat. I walked to a deck chair by the railing and sat facing the party. I took a large sip of gin and got bearings on my navigational aides: Hutch, the tallest of the guests, was teaching a dance step to a handsome elderly woman wearing pants who looked at him as though he were Zeus; Mom carried a tray of deviled eggs across the porch, followed by a red-faced man focused on her ass. The bartender was mixing herself a drink. With a crowd surrounding him, Old Man Wendell, still in full Indian-chief regalia, pantomimed himself beside home plate with an imaginary baseball bat in his hand. He pointed to the pretend fans in center field, then swung away and, using the entire porch as his infield, rounded the bases. Men and women along his route slapped him high-fives. His red chest was damp, the headdress had pitched forward but was still hanging on, and he pointed a single finger toward the sky. As he crossed home plate, three young women slowed his momentum so he wouldn't barrel off the porch and onto the rocks; they all held him closely and one of them, wearing a blue sundress, combed her fingers through his white hair.

Mom came over to me and leaned against the railing. Her hair stood up in the humidity and she looked the way she had when I came back from summer camp, almost twenty years ago. "Sweetie," she said. "Are you surviving?"

"I love this," I said.

She hugged me, and when she was letting go she slipped a note into my pants pocket. "Read this in private," she whispered. "I love you, sweetie." She walked back to the swirl of the crowd.

I took a big sip of gin, checked my watch, and looked up to see that the bartender was gone. I went to the stairs, descended slowly (I wasn't drunk, but I had to will myself not to stumble), and walked on a trail through chest-high bushes of bay winding to a spot under the porch where large pillars kept the house from collapsing into the ocean. She was waiting.

"Precious," she said. "Come here."

She hugged me and put her hand on my cheek.

"I've missed you," I said. I wasn't lying, really. She put her face against my chest and squeezed tighter.

"You're so sweet, even though you're bad," she said.

"I won't be bad anymore," I said. "I'm Mr. Goody-goody from now on."

"You won't be," she said. "But I'll forgive you." She unbuckled my belt and I pulled her shirt over her head and when she had my pants down around my ankles, she pulled my face to her chest. She went to work on me with her left hand.

"Jesus," I said, marveling at this turn of events.

"Wait," she said. "I hear someone." She put her shirt on and walked to the corner of the house, peered around it, then slipped out of sight. I didn't move from where I was, I just bent down and pulled up my jeans, buttoned them and looked out at the ocean above the tops of the bay bushes.

When she came back, she was carrying a handgun. She handed it to me like it was a dirty sock.

"Hold this," she said, leaning over and kissing me. The kiss, at least, didn't confuse me. She pressed into me, held her lips against mine, and when she released me I kissed her again. "I need to go back to the bar," she said. Her cheeks were flushed. Then she took the gun out of my hand and tucked it into the back of my jeans. "Keep it here. Everything will be fine," she said.

"What?" I asked.

"They'll get suspicious if I stay down here too long," she said, walking toward the stairs. "My brother will find you. He'll explain."

"Wait," I said, but she was gone and I had no choice but to buckle my belt. The voices from the party were loud, even filtered through the deck boards, and what sounded like a swing band had started playing. I looked at the woods and thought about running. I was nostalgic for home. Then I found myself breathing deeply and walking back up to the porch.

The band included two trombones, a trumpet, a clarinet, stand-up bass, kettle drums, a piano, a guitar. The old man was in the thick of the dancing, spinning with his arms raised in the middle of a group. The party had grown; there was now a greater variety of costumes. I saw an Egyptian princess and a lion tamer. Many people were waiting to get drinks from my bartender. I stared at her, and just as she was finishing two scotch and sodas for the next two people in line, she looked over at me and winked, and I panicked. She seemed so whole-hearted, so loving, and her legs were very long; I considered my shortcomings and worried that I would fail.

There was a gun, probably loaded, in the back of my pants. I guessed that I could point it if I had to. Hutch and Mom were dancing together, and they had all the steps; from time to time he would pick her up and use his body as a fulcrum to fling her from side to side. It was impressive, and Mom kept up. The song was Benny Goodman's "Sing, Sing, Sing." It had the party in a frenzy—there were even a few small children running back and forth on the porch, and I saw a man inadvertently trip a young boy who then fell on his face but got right back up and started running again. I walked inside the house.

When I entered the foyer, a man and a woman dressed in saris passed quickly in front of me, each carrying a silver tray of warm scallops. They both gave me a friendly smile and a nod. At the bottom of a wide staircase stood a ten-foot-high mirror; I checked to make sure the gun wasn't visible. Then I headed to the second floor, two stairs at a time.

The landing was without furniture, a large open space leading to various bedrooms. There were a few large portraits, each painted with a dark background, each lit from below with an individual light. The ceilings were higher than I was used to. The largest of the portraits was of the old man, but in the painting he was younger and he was seated at a large wooden desk.

I heard someone coming up the stairs but kept my gaze on the painting. When he arrived at the top of the stairs, he spoke.

"Isn't that a damn great picture?" he asked. "It's when he was governor."

He came up next to me holding two drinks, and he handed me one. He was the size of an offensive lineman, had black hair cropped short, and wore a white suit, like a naval officer. "He looks young," I said.

"Leila didn't tell you much, did she," he said.

"You mean down at the bar?" I asked.

"Yes, I mean down at the bar," he said. "*Leila.*" He seemed angry.

"No, not much," I said.

"Not much *what?*"

"She didn't tell me much," I said.

"Christ. She doesn't do well with these kinds of things. She gets overly sentimental." He wiped his mouth with his hand. "The old man has pancreatic cancer. They told him four months ago he had three months to live."

"Damn," I said.

"You know your cancers, buddy?" he asked.

"Not really," I said.

"You know what the pancreas does?" he asked.

I shook my head.

"It's in the thick of things, in there," he said, poking me hard in the gut. "This kind of cancer messes you up. Bad. He's already getting the pain and the vomiting and it's spreading to his other organs. He won't do chemo. You know why not?"

I shook my head.

"'Cause he's a madman. I admire him for it, but he's a staunch bastard. We've finally gotten him on some heroin. Before, he was just gritting his teeth through the pain."

"He sounds tough," I said.

"You're goddamned right he is. Now, because it's his birthday and he wasn't supposed to make it this far, he asked that we throw him a bash, like the old Augusta blowouts, and he asked that at midnight we shoot him dead."

I stared at him. He didn't waver.

"We figure you're the best guy to do it," he said, slapping a hand on my shoulder.

"I've never even shot a gun," I said.

He pulled up my shirt and took the gun from the back of my pants. "It's pretty basic. Point and pull. You've seen movies." He aimed the pistol at the portrait of the old man, said "Bang" and faked the recoil, then blew imaginary smoke from the barrel.

"You try," he said, handing me the gun.

I put it back in my pants. "I don't think I'll be killing your grandfather," I said.

"Listen. It's what he wants. You're not going to get locked up for it. Everyone's counting on you—they've all agreed to it, even his wife. Leila wants you to do it, too. Right now the old man's so crocked he won't feel a thing."

"Do you not think this is a very odd thing to be asking me?"

He looked at me as though I were crazy. "Settle down, buddy," he said.

"How about giving me a minute to think," I said. "Okay? I need a second to think."

"The name's Tilly," he said, rubbing his short hair, then extending his hand. Like the other handshakes, it was firm and long-lasting. "I know Leila didn't give you much of a chance to acclimate yourself. That's her style." Then he raised his glass. "To the family," he said.

We clinked our drinks together; then he walked down the stairs.

I took the note my mother had given me out of my pocket. It said:

IT'S OKAY.

IT'S HOW THINGS ARE DONE HERE.

YOU'RE THE BEST!   —MOM

I raised the drink again, this time in the direction of the old man's portrait, and drank it down. Then I set the glass on the floor, felt for the gun, and walked downstairs.

On the porch, the moon had risen, and torches had been lighted along the railing. I thought about Augusta, the old days of Governor Wendell. I walked to the bar, where Leila was already pouring my gin. I leaned over and kissed her wetly— my excitement had me making the gestures of a movie star— and she grabbed my wrist and held me. "I love you," she said.

The band was on break; they stood by the railing drinking bottled beer and smoking. I took a spoon from the bar and with my gin and tonic in hand walked to a chair and stepped onto the railing. I felt a slight dizziness and nearly fell over onto the rocks, but I got my footing. I was standing well above the crowd when I started clinking my glass with the spoon.

There were probably a hundred people in attendance, all relatives of the old man, most of them sweating from the dancing and the drinking, all of them looking brightly up at me.

It got quiet quickly.

"Hello," I said. I wasn't much of a public speaker, but I felt strong. "I want to introduce myself." There were cries of "Hear, hear!" from some of the people, and I had a fondness for them. "There's been some confusion about who I am," I continued, my voice louder than I'd expected. "My name's Roger. I'm a bartender in Portland. This is my first time in Point Allison."

More "Hear, hear!"s followed. Some clapped, and there were whistles, too. "I'm glad to be here with Leila"— and I raised my glass to her. She was standing by the bar at the far end of the porch, and she beamed. "And with Tilly," I said, keeping the glass raised. He raised his own glass and bellowed, "To a new brother!" and a great cheer rose throughout the party. Again, I nearly toppled off the railing. "Also," I said, when it got quiet, "to Hutch and my mom—to their life together." This, too, was a popular choice, evoking many more "Hear, hear!"s. Hutch and Mom were standing together, arm in arm, their clothes clinging to their bodies from the Benny Goodman. "And finally," I said, nearly yelling now, caught up in the emotion of it all, "to the old man!" A roaring "Hooray!" began, and as the cheering continued, I spotted him across the way, standing by the bar. The cheering turned to a kind of chanting—"Hup! Hup! Hup!"—with many of the partygoers stomping their feet on the porch. The motion caused me to sway back and forth on the railing; when people saw this, they settled down. "Thank you for having me. I'm sorry a toast is all I can offer."

This didn't go over as well. There was a frightening silence, and then a murmuring. The sea of people began to part between me and the old man. He was standing there, quietly combing the feathers of his headdress back, preening them. Then he picked up the knife used for lime slicing on the bar, and he was charging toward me. It was a long run across the porch, and his cry started low—"Errr"—and ended high— "Ahhhh!" He stopped just short of me, with the large blade raised in his hand like a scythe; he might have swept down and taken off my legs like shoots of wheat, but I had the gun out and was pointing it at him.

Then he screamed again and swung the knife, and I shot him in the chest.

He was blown back, flat on his back—an explosion of crimson on his bare chest—and he lay there, still, while everyone stood waiting, shocked by the drama of it all. The torch flames snapped in the wind. Hutch raised his hands and began to clap over his head, and the others followed, and the stiff applause turned into bellowing and hooting, much more raucous than it had been before.

$$\Big[\qquad \text{R{\scriptsize IDE}} \qquad \Big]$$

I{\scriptsize N HIS ROOM AT HOME, ALDEN KEEPS A PICTURE OF HIS} dad wearing hunting clothes, yellow and brown brush camouflage print with bloodstains on the knees. He's standing in a field, leaning against an old car that's been abandoned there, a large black sedan from the forties propped up on its axles. He rests against the car holding four woodcock, two in each hand. The sky hangs gray and the grass in the field is matted down flat. His shotgun, barrel open, lies on the hood of the car. His cheeks are red and his sideburns are long and full.

They're in the Adirondacks now, headed to Plattsburgh, New York, in his dad's forty-foot Freightliner. Looking at his watch, his dad pulls the airhorn at exactly midnight, bleeding the tanks until the pressure alarm goes off. Alden holds his hands over his ears. He tries to follow the noise as it travels through the woods, reflects off cliffs, wakes up animals, and comes to rest someplace far away—by a frozen pond, maybe, or in a field of snow.

"There it is," his dad says. "Happy birthday."

As they accelerate through curves, Alden can feel the truck's trailer hanging empty behind them—a spotless chamber which his father calls "the chapel." All they're hauling is a pine crate, suitcase-sized, which is strapped to the back wall. His father's voice, the smell of tobacco and sweat and potato chips and coffee—all of this feels immediate and slightly unreal. He hasn't lived with his dad for a long time—his parents split eight years ago.

"Aldie," his dad says, lighting a Winston and squeezing it in his lips, inhaling deeply. "Sixteen—that's a big one. It's when you take off the training wheels."

WHEN HIS FATHER ASKED HIM TO GO ON THE TRIP, HE COULD have said no politely, apologetically, as he had many times in the past, but Alden was beginning to see the advantages of time spent with his father. They'd gotten to the point where they were so unknown to each other that their visits felt adventurous. They'd eat together maybe twice a year, when his father was running a job up I-95. His dad would call a day ahead, and they'd meet at the Miss Somesville Diner, where his father would tell stories and Alden would order a steak, laugh at the right times, pretend to be a man. His mother drove him to the diner, always deciding at the last minute how much time Alden could spend there—sometimes two hours, sometimes only forty-five minutes. When his time was up, she'd be waiting in her car at the edge of the parking lot, near the newspaper vending machines. It had been nine months since he'd last seen his father, and this time, his dad suggested they meet in New York, run a job upstate, then spend his birthday together. Alden said yes right away.

His father picked him up just outside Grand Central Station, and they'd driven the Freightliner up Madison Avenue, passing polished granite facades, gold and mirrored storefronts, before turning on Eighty-third Street toward Central Park, rolling down a ramp to the Metropolitan Museum's loading dock. There, men in white smocks and cotton gloves ducked under lowering gates. Phones were ringing in every direction. Two security guards with guns in their holsters were stooped over, rolling a small pine box onto the Freightliner. On each side of the box, the museum had stamped the word EXCLUSIVE in two-inch red letters, meaning it was a point-to-point job, during which no other deliveries could be made. Underneath these letters, someone had written "RAMSEY, WILLIAM. PLATTSBURGH, NEW YORK."

"Maybe it's the Mona Lisa," his dad said, winking.

THEY ARE JUST AN HOUR FROM PLATTSBURGH WHEN SNOW begins to swirl on the windshield. The rainbow of dashboard gauges—fluorescent reds, oranges, and greens—glows off his father's face, and the heating unit for the trailer rumbles above them. Alden feels full of hope, because it's warm in the cab, and the road is smooth and well lit by the headlights, and he anticipates stopping for junk food—all those truck-stop choices thrill him, even when he's not hungry. Also, his ass doesn't hurt yet. And it's his birthday.

The only catch is that he's not comfortable shooting the breeze with his dad—the diner is an easier venue. There, his father could entertain Alden by flirting with the waitress, for which his dad's strategy was always the same. He'd ask her to sit down on the stool next to them when she took their order, and if she was young, he'd ask where she went to high school, and he'd pretend to know her teachers if she mentioned their names. If she was older, he'd ask about her kids, and maybe even her husband. "You can relax with us," he'd say. "We won't make you work too hard."

In the truck, where there are fewer distractions, Alden is forced to make conversation. He asks, "You remember being sixteen?"

"Well," he says, smiling, "the thing was, I was built for that age. I lived on my own and I didn't have very many concerns. I washed dishes for my rent money." His dad has a tendency to speak this way, as though he were answering questions on a talk show.

"Where'd you wash dishes?"

"You know. One of those places."

Then it's quiet again. Alden glances at his father, at his graying red hair and the wrinkles where he squints.

It's hard for Alden to believe they were in the city earlier that day—it feels like weeks ago. Alden stares at the lines on the highway, unwavering in the truck's supercharged headlights.

"You should have seen how many Botero sculptures I hauled last week, Aldie," his dad says. "Thing is, a Botero is like a Buick, and I hauled fourteen of the suckers. They're these big shiny black sculptures. They're all really fat. His birds are fat, and he makes fat ladies, fat cats, fat kings and queens. If he does a dog, it's this massive thing, as big as an elephant. It's a simple equation. I envy the man. I mean, God bless him, people love his work. I think it's because these big fat things are so recognizable—which means even dumb fuckers can say, 'Oh look! It's a Botero.' Maybe I should have been an artist. Those sculptures are worth a fortune." He lights a cigarette.

"I thought you wanted to be a hit man," says Alden. So far on the trip, his father has said he'd make a shrewd lawyer, an enterprising manager of a fast food restaurant, one hell of an astronaut.

"It would be perfect, really. No one would expect that from me," he says, laughing. "Your mother might expect it, but she's the only one. She knows what I'm capable of." What his mother has told Alden is that she loved him, but that he was too much of a dreamer, too stubborn to live with. Whenever she speaks of him, Alden knows she's holding a lot back. He remembers when he was eight, his father decided he'd make his fortune by raising llamas, and that for a while he had seventeen of them, which he kept in a rented paddock in Point Allison. He would go on and on about the virtues of the species, lecturing Alden and his mother at the dinner table. They're smart and independent and they have an uncanny sense of personal space, he'd say. His mother hated this talk, Alden remembers, and when seven of them died of a rare blood disorder and his father sold a necklace of hers to buy five more, that was it. He was gone two months later. The llama episode is the main reason his mother doesn't want Alden to spend time with him; she doesn't want Alden to pick up any of his habits.

Without announcement, his father exits the highway onto a thinner road. When they veer down into a hollow, near a stream that parallels the road, it's easy to feel how light the truck is, how empty. The brakes don't strain on the downhill, and a small burst of diesel heaves them up the other side. The trailer leans against the turns.

With all the dips and curves, Alden can tell they're in the mountains, but he can't see the peaks—they're hidden by the forest, and by the snow, which is falling much more heavily now. Alden remembers reading somewhere that the Adirondacks are an old mountain range, older than the Rockies, big windswept piles of granite. This gives him an empty, paralyzed feeling, all those old rocks, like the time he saw a late-night show on the Pyramids and couldn't get his head around the idea of all those Egyptians being dead for thousands of years. He tries to shake the thought by imagining the next truck stop—racks and racks of quilted plaid shirts, Silhouette Lady mud flaps, biker magnets, Road Warrior sew-on patches. A smorgasbord of beef jerky.

"You ever talk to people when you're on the road?" asks Alden.

"How do you mean?"

"If you're at a truck stop, or at a restaurant, or—I don't know, wherever—you ever chat people up, get to know them?"

asks Alden. He wonders this about his dad—he's never heard about his friends, and the only people he's watched him talk to are waitresses.

"Sometimes I talk to people. A lot of the time, though, it's just a letdown. When you think about it, there aren't many people out there worth knowing."

They pass a sign announcing the Elizabethtown Motel and Restaurant: COME TO WHERE THE COMFORT IS! Alden sees mobile homes in the periphery of the headlights, dark rectangles strewn irregularly by the side of the highway. His father downshifts and begins to slow the truck. Up ahead there's a package store with gas pumps, but the lights are out.

"I think it's closed," says Alden.

"Yup," says his dad. Alden can feel the truck sliding in the snow, and his father eases off the brakes. He pulls up next to the diesel pumps, which are dark. The store has a porch in front, with a phone booth.

"I guess you're old enough to get all the details on this," his father says. "You okay with that?"

"Sure," says Alden.

"That's just because you have no idea what I'm talking about," he says, exhaling, pushing a hand through his hair.

"What?"

"Well, give me a second, for Christ sake."

"Okay," says Alden.

"Here's the thing. We're going to wait at this store for a guy I know. He's going to help us with this job. Help us get this painting we're hauling up to Canada."

"It's not going to Plattsburgh?"

"Nope. It's supposed to be going there. But that's where the old man gets smart." He turns off the engine. "What we're going to do is make it look like we've been held up." He glances at his watch. "Williamson's supposed to be here by now."

"How?"

His father looks annoyed. "He's driving his car down from Montreal."

"I mean how are you going to make it look like we've been held up?"

"We don't really have to do anything. We just have to tell them that someone crazy put a gun to my head."

Alden's confused. "Why'd you stop at this store in the first place?"

"It's where we're meeting Williamson."

"I know. But why . . . you know . . . in the story you're going to tell the cops?"

"It doesn't matter. Maybe I'll tell them I didn't think it was closed."

"And that the robbers just happened to be here?"

"Hell, it doesn't matter. I'm not supposed to know any-thing, right? If I have some elaborate theory, the cops will smell that, right? Maybe the robbers were following me. Maybe they were following me all the way from New York."

"Oh," says Alden.

"And don't you worry. This money's for you. It's not all for me, you know. I've been paying every bill your mom sends me for the last eight years, that's been fine. But now I want to set us up for a while, okay?"

His father clicks on the radio.

"Have you ever done this before?" asks Alden.

"You think that matters?" says his dad.

"No, not really. I'm just curious."

"Well, it does matter. Because no, I haven't done it before, which is probably what'll make it work."

Alden opens his door and gets out. He looks up in the sky, closes his eyes, and feels the big snowflakes against his face, in his eyelashes. None of what's happening feels real. It doesn't seem dangerous, or exciting. Already it feels like a story he'll be telling his mom. With his eyes closed, he wants to see only darkness but he sees flashes of light, though when he opens his eyes again, it's the same quiet scene, almost pretty in the snow: this dead store, the faint sound of country music coming from the truck.

Then the pay phone rings, which seems impossible. He looks at his father, who sits unmoving in the truck, listening to the music. Two more rings go by before Alden goes to the truck, opens the door on his father's side and says, "This phone out here is ringing."

"Why don't you get it?" says his father.

"I want you to pick it up," says Alden.

"Jesus," says his father, hopping down from his seat into the snow, then running over to the phone. He talks for only a few seconds, then slams the phone down. He jogs back to the truck.

"Okay," he says. "He went off the road outside La Prairie. We need to take it up to Canada ourselves."

•   •   •

ALDEN HAS NEVER BEEN OUTSIDE THE UNITED STATES, AND while he has little faith in his father's plan, he likes the idea of crossing into foreign territory. Twenty minutes later, they're at the border, driving under a row of tall, pooling fluorescent lights. They roll up to a booth at the same level as the truck's cab, high above the road. Low scrub and dwarfed trees cover the land around them, and the lights make everything sharp.

"Aldie," his dad says, sighing. "This is what we call a D-plus operation—real junior varsity." His mother says he gets this way sometimes because he thinks he knows how things should be done correctly—it's the marine in him. Even when waiting in line at the DMV, or going to the town hall to get a burn permit, it's the exact same thing.

"Bonjour, hello," says the woman in the booth, without looking up. "United States citizens, both of you?" Her well-enunciated English is fringed by an accent.

"This is my son here. Sixteen years old today. Well, yes, we're both Americans. Yes ma'am," his dad says, handing her the truck papers.

"And what are you bringing to Canada?" she asks.

His father glances at Alden, then turns back toward the woman. "Military dominance," he says. "Louisiana jazz, Fenway Park, the Chevy Silverado." Then, after a dramatic pause, "The Grand Canyon." He laughs. "Just kidding, Ma'am, of course."

Alden has heard this list, and others like it, before. The woman is wearing a tan uniform and looks about his mom's age; she has sharp eyebrows and short brown hair. "Excuse me?"

"We're empty, ma'am," he says. "We're going up to Montreal to get some seafood."

"Sir, the climate-control unit for your trailer is engaged," she says. She sounds relaxed, with the calm assurance you get when you have the authority of an entire country behind you.

"Is it, ma'am?" his dad asks.

"Full blast," she says.

"I better turn it off. Don't want to heat something that's not back there."

"On the left, there, is Import," she says, pointing. "Back into loading dock three and open your trailer. An officer will be with you shortly."

Alden's father releases the air brake, and they roll from the window. "That's the other thing I'm bringing to Canada," he says. "A goddamn sense of humor."

They pull into Import, open the trailer doors, and back their way into a loading dock. Alden is out in the cold, giving hand signals. Flapping of the hand means keep coming, straight ahead; then he holds his hands apart, showing his dad how much room there is before his bumper meets the dock. With its own diesel engine fed by the main fuel tanks, the reefer unit on the Freightliner is a workhorse. It pumps hot air from the trailer into the loading dock.

His dad sets the air brakes, a loud crack, then a hiss. Now the snow is falling in a fine mist, a spray of sugar. It's cold weather snow, the kind that could last for days. The seam between the trailer and the Import bay leaks some heat to Alden, so he stands close. Up by the cab, he sees his dad's shoulder in the long vertical mirror. He jogs up to the cab and climbs in the passenger side.

"Aldie, I need you to keep lookout for me. Go wait on the slab back there. I'm going to get that crate from the chapel."

"That seems like a bad idea," says Alden.

"Like you would know? They won't see anything, Aldie. Don't worry."

"I say we turn around now, Dad. Before this gets any worse."

"Come on now," his dad says, pleading. "It's not your ass, it's mine."

The parking lot by Import is one of the best-lit places Alden has ever seen. There are lampposts—tall, as bright as light-house lanterns—every fifteen feet. The snow is filling the air now, churning, and the sky is thick black above the tops of the lampposts. The snow falls brightly by the bulbs, and as the light spreads out toward the ground, the snow is less visible, but three or four inches have already fallen. He gets out of the truck.

The snow burns his arms but feels good in his hair, which is hot from the heat of the cab. He walks back to the end of the truck and stands by the warm draft again. There's a truck in the next bay, and two men sit on the separating concrete slab. They speak a singsong version of French, lots of ups and downs. Instead of "oui," they say "whey." They're laughing loudly, shaking, occasionally clapping their hands. One of them is wearing a black wool hat which fits tightly on his head, and the other has pockmarked skin and gray spiked hair. They are smoking cigarettes with gloves on.

"Bonjour," Alden says to them.

"Hello," the one with the spiked hair says, and his companion nods, silently.

"Great spot," says Alden.

"Whey," they both say, laughing some more and nodding. The guy with spiked hair says, "It gets even better when Mr. Immigration comes here, sticks his gun in your guts, and blows off your kidneys."

This makes both the men laugh again. There's no burning on Alden's arms anymore, they're numb. The one with the gray spiked hair takes a fresh cigarette out of his pack and points it in Alden's direction.

"Merci," Alden says, extending a pink arm that doesn't feel part of him. Then the man walks up to his cab and comes back with a plaid wool shirt and gloves.

"You from Florida, tough man?" he says as he hands Alden the clothes. The one in the hat says something in French to the one with spiked hair—it seems he doesn't like that these clothes have been offered to Alden. But they say nothing more, so while holding the cigarette in his mouth, Alden puts on the shirt and the gloves—which smell like air freshener, something floral.

"Maine. I'm just catching a ride with this guy," he says, pointing toward his father's truck. "I've been on the road for a few days."

"Does he stop to let you take a piss?" asks the man with spiked hair. "Because Reggie, he doesn't stop to let me piss." Alden looks at Reggie, who is smiling with his arms folded across his chest.

"He lets me," says Alden.

"Well, mister, you're one lucky bastard," says the man with spiked hair.

Alden hasn't smoked many cigarettes before, and this one burns stale and strong. He tries not to inhale too much until he's gotten used to the smoke in his mouth. Ready, he sucks deep, holds it, then opens his mouth and lets it drift thick over his teeth. His eyes water and his vision changes and he almost falls over, but he realizes he hasn't moved. The snow coming into the loading dock is gentle, landing on heads and mustaches silently. Alden looks back out at the lampposts, shining as brilliantly as ever, then tosses the cigarette into the snow, where it blackens. Again he sees his dad's shoulder in the vertical mirror. His dad opens the door and waves Alden up to the cab.

"Christ. They might have seen me," his dad says. His face is red from the heat of the cab, and from the excitement. "I saw where the camera was, and I stayed out of its way. But then somebody came out onto the . . . " He stops, wrinkling his nose. "Aldie, were you smoking?" he asks.

"Nope. Those guys back there, they lent me this shirt," he says, still pumped with nicotine.

"Aldie, we need to take control of the situation," his father says, out of breath. "That's exactly what we're going to do. It's what you and I are, Aldie. We're take-control types. You're sixteen, bub—time to show the world what you're made of." Alden feels the pine suitcase behind his seat, where it's lodged, hidden.

The Immigration officer is in the back of the truck. Alden hears his boots. His dad puts a Winston in his teeth and lights it. A minute later, the officer's at the window.

"Extinguish the cigarette," the officer says. He has a foot-long silver flashlight which he shines in Alden's eyes. "What's your business in Canada?" he asks.

"Just visiting," Alden's dad says.

"Sir, let me tell you something about my job," says the officer. He has a neatly trimmed moustache and a thin mouth. "I'm cold and I'm tired. I'm at the end of my twelve-hour shift. You're not in Canada yet. You're with me, and you'll answer me directly."

"What I was going to tell you—"

"Am I clear?"

"—is that we're picking up some artwork in Canada."

"Am I clear?"

"Sure," his father says. "You're clear."

"The next shift will do the cab inspection. Officer McKenna will be with you shortly."

His father sighs. "Jesus, you're not going to take a knife to my seats, are you? I've had that done by you guys before."

"Stay in the cab," says the officer. Then he walks away.

"Have a wonderful evening," says his father, after the officer has left.

He hops out of the cab and Alden follows him. They walk into the Import lobby, which is lit only by vending machines and a red glowing exit sign. Alden scans a humming candy machine: every dispenser is filled with the same kind of toffee. His dad goes to the pay phone, and Alden heads for the men's room.

The floor by the toilets is muddy from boots and urine. There's no heat in the bathroom; his breath steams and the sink fixtures are painfully cold. Alden looks at his face in the mirror. His skin is white but his nose stands out pink. Sixteen, he says to himself. A cigarette-smoking, French-speaking son of a blundering outlaw.

Alden walks out of the bathroom, and through the window he sees the other truck pull out of Import, and as it turns, the rear wheels of the trailer slide across the snow-covered asphalt, fishtailing gently. Then the trailer pulls straight.

Alden walks past his father, and when he gets outside he jogs across the lot toward the moving truck. In the snow, it's silent. Alden sees its brake lights flash—a bright, hopeful red— then his feet come out from under him and he lands hard on the asphalt, first his elbows, then the right side of his ribs, then his right knee. He reminds himself it would have hurt much more had there not been snow—but then again, he wouldn't have slipped had the asphalt been dry. The truck is idling, waiting for him. He runs to the passenger side, where the man with spiked hair has rolled down the window.

"Nice stunt back there," says the man, laughing. "Très bien."

"I didn't give you back your stuff," says Alden.

"No?" he says. "That's okay, those things are Reggie's." He jabs a thumb in his partner's direction.

Alden hears a spill of French words from Reggie, whom he can't see.

"Oh, what a generous guy," says the man, laughing. "Reggie says you can have them. He found them in the trash at a truck stop in Iberville."

"You guys have space?" asks Alden. "It's fine if you don't, I can wait, but that other rig's being delayed, and I'm hoping to keep moving."

"No problem, we can give you a ride," he says. "You ride in the trailer, okay? You fit back there. It's dark, but we have only one hour before Montreal. It's good back there, plenty of room."

"Sounds fine," says Alden.

The man opens his door and swings his legs around, then hops down out of the cab, landing quietly on the snow. He walks with Alden to the back of the truck, where he opens the padlock and one of the hinged doors. "I'll give you a second to find your way, then I close you up," he says. "Take a good look around before it gets dark."

Inside the trailer doors are three tall lamps strapped to the wall, a grandfather clock, a bookshelf, four mattresses on their sides, stacked together. The rest of the stuff inside is too far back to see. Alden puts a foot on the bumper, and just as he's pulling himself up, he hears a high whistle from across the parking lot. He looks toward the Import bay and sees his father, waving him back. He stares at his father, who then starts waving with greater urgency.

"Oh," says Alden. "Looks like he's ready now. Maybe I'll just go with him."

"Okay," says the man, who slams the door closed.

"Sorry," says Alden.

The man clicks the padlock shut. "Hey, he lets you stop to piss, right?" says the man. "You're better off, mon frère." The man walks back up to the cab, hops inside, and the truck pulls away.

When Alden gets back to the Import dock, he gets into his

father's truck and his father leans toward him. "You wouldn't believe it," he whispers, smiling. "These guys are total amateurs. This last Gomer looks behind the seat, sees the crate, doesn't even ask me what's in it."

"Oh yeah?"

"Must have thought it was a toolbox. I didn't even flinch, Aldie. Not one bit."

His father releases the air brakes and pulls slowly out of the bay. "I talked to Williamson again," says his father. "He called it off. I guess there's no reason to push it tonight." Then he carves a large U-turn. At the American gate, they roll up to a booth where an officer with an American flag on his shoulder has his chin down on his chest with his eyes closed. Alden has forgotten about the time, but he figures it must be nearly three in the morning.

"I missed my exit, back down in Plattsburgh," his dad says.

"One minute," the officer says. He mutters a few words into an intercom mounted to the wall, clicking it with his thumb, looking absently at the truck. Then he says, "You were just headed into Canada?"

"No, sir," says his father.

"You weren't just headed into Canada," says the man.

"Yes," says Alden, almost too loudly. "Into Canada. Yes sir."

"Yes?" asks the officer.

"We were, but the pickup got canceled," says Alden. "They called it off because of the weather."

"Sir?" asks the officer.

Alden's father nods and says, "That's right."

"Sorry for the mixup, sir," says Alden.

"I recommend you get off the road soon, with all this snow," says the officer.

"Will do," says Alden.

"Go ahead," says the officer, waving them on.

Any snow that momentarily settles in the spruce trees soon swirls up in gusts of wind. Then his father lights a Winston. "Let me do the talking next time," he says, finally. He breathes out smoke like a sleuth.

"I didn't want you to mess things up again," says Alden.

"Oh, thank you *so much*," his dad says. "Thanks for saving me, son. You're my savior."

"Just so you know," says Alden, "I was saving myself, not you." He says this without thinking, and it makes him go numb, so he squeezes his arms and tries to stare at the lines on the highway again. He and his father are quiet for the rest of the trip.

When they arrive at the motel, his father puts the pine box in the trailer and keeps the heater running.

The room is dimly lit, the wallpaper is watercolored deer and moose standing in brown and yellow reeds. There is only one bed, king-size, and Alden climbs into it next to his father. When they turn out the lamp, light from the parking lot glows through the curtains. In the faint light of the room, he catches a glimpse of his father, who has the sheets pulled up into his armpits, his arms resting above the covers. His father says, "I guess your birthday didn't work out quite like I planned. I was thinking we'd rent some skates in Montreal. Go out on the river."

"It's all right," says Alden.

"Next time," says his father.

"Okay," says Alden, but Alden knows any chance of this happening has past.

Then his father sits up, clicks on the lamp. "I have an idea," he says. In his white briefs, he pulls on his boots, grabs his keys, and opens the door to the motel room. Then he walks out into the snow. In a few minutes, he's back, pink-chested, clutching the pine box under one arm. He lays it on the bed, unscrewing the side of it with a Swiss Army knife on his key chain. He removes the panel, slips the painting from its foam sheath, then removes the glassine wrapping.

Alden props a few pillows behind his head and watches as his dad, in boots and underwear, places the painting in front of the TV.

A tree frog fills most of the canvas—it's huge and wet-looking, settled in the grass. The sun on its back makes its skin appear white. The frog isn't realistic, but the light is. "Jesus," says his father. "That's some crazy shit right there."

"You like it?" asks Alden.

"I like it fine," says his father. "You?"

"Sure."

"Not what I was expecting, but still pretty nice. I was convinced it was going to be something else."

"The Mona Lisa?" asks Alden.

"Hey, don't be a smart-ass," says his dad, with his arms folded on his chest, staring at the painting. "I was ninety-nine percent sure it was this little Cézanne number, with apples in it."

"Good thing you didn't steal this one," says Alden.

"You got that right, soldier," says his father.

"I mean, the frog's pretty good, but if you weren't expecting it—"

"—it's a whole different operation. Right you are," says his father. "Hey, maybe we should go up to Canada anyway. Tomorrow. Just for the hell of it."

"I'm ready to get home," says Alden.

"Okay," says his father, staring intently at the painting. "I guess it's time to get some sleep." He climbs back under the covers. After turning off the lamp for the second time he says, "Well, happy birthday."

"Thanks," says Alden, and in the dark he listens for the truck's heating unit, but it's off now.

As he tries to sleep, Alden remembers the day when his father left Maine—he had taken Alden out for breakfast, though he can't remember the conversation. Alden suspects his dad had been apologetic. He had to have been. And Alden went with him to Point Allison, to get the money for the llamas—he'd sold them. (Alden remembers the llamas, perhaps not from that particular visit to Point Allison, but he remembers the way they walked slowly in their paddock, looking curious and dignified.) And then there was the moment when his dad pressed the money into Alden's hand, a small smooth fold of bills, asking him to deliver it to Alden's mother. He had liked that. He hadn't known the full meaning of the gesture, but he knew it was a good thing, that it would improve the situation, and he liked that he could be the deliverer. He liked being a part of the exchange. Alden doesn't know when he'd started to home in on loneliness. It had snuck up on him, really. (He used to feel a touch of surprise when he looked at himself in the mirror, as though most of the time he was unaware he was separate from the rest of the world.) In some ways, this feels right—in the daytime, he is invigorated by solitude. But in the motel room, he just feels lonely. With his father sleeping next to him, Alden feels a new kind of sadness, as though he's got a secret which he will never tell.

[Cuxabexis, Cuxabexis]

On the ferry, Eleanor reclines in a plastic seat bolted to the linoleum floor with her feet resting on a suitcase. Bill sits next to her, by the window, legs crossed, silver glasses crammed against his face—scanning the *Courier-Gazette*. She has never been on a boat before, but then again, she has never before been pregnant, either—she is six-weeks in—so she's not sure which is contributing most to her mood. She is irritated with Bill. Doesn't he know he should be feeding her? He should know she needs meat. The issue is rarely quantity of food, or variety—it's access. And she imagines there won't be anything to eat on the island, which will be Bill's fault.

"Meat," she says.

"Yes?"

"That's what I need."

He doesn't raise his eyes from the paper. "This boat doesn't have a snack bar."

"But I saw vending machines," she says. He looks up at her and smiles, and this angers her at first, but his smile lingers and his glasses are so round—his nostrils are flared in a ridiculous manner—that despite her efforts, she can't be annoyed. "Sit tight," he says. He folds the paper and sets it on the floor. "I'll check the Coke machine for hamburgers." He steps over her legs, and as he walks from the passenger cabin—his shoes snapping on the linoleum—she watches his ass, his dress shirt tucked neatly into his wool slacks.

Then, the thought descends: this is not how it's always been. She is different than she once was. How simple an idea that is! Just a few years ago, her life had been stacked in three neat piles. For money, she waited tables—at a place called Enrique's on the Upper West Side. Seven shifts a week: three lunches, four dinners. Bring the people their food. Ask polite questions about what is needed. Grit teeth. Balance drinks on a tray. Run credit card through machine; smack machine and run card again. After work, there was action sometimes. She had various sleep-over friends, men who didn't bother her otherwise—one she knew from college, one she worked with at the restaurant, one she'd met at the library. Then there had been her schoolwork—never a problem. The prize was entrance to medical school, Columbia.

But things have slipped. Eleanor loves her brain, but she has started to saturate. In medical school, she has learned that everything can and will go wrong with a body, and that too many of the drugs she is studying—of various synthetic origins—cause hives, breathing difficulty, and dizziness. There is so much to learn. (Surgery has been better: she likes to cut, and the muscle-flexing culture of surgeons amuses her.) After she stopped seeing her sleep-over friends, she met Bill.

Bill is from Maine. Bill is from Cuxabexis Island—though he lives in Boston now. And he is off looking for meat, for her. It's March and the clouds are low and the water is hazel, the color of Bill's eyes. It's snowing. Looking at the water gives Eleanor the feeling she gets at the end of a long shift on her surgical rotation, a weakness in her abdomen and legs—fatigued from remembering, and from the actual labor of cutting, or watching the doctors cut. The water looks very solid and thick, and she finds it hard to imagine all that's below her; she fears falling and sinking, hypothermic shock, being swept by the tide onto the shore of a barren reef, ice in her hair, matted with seaweed. She's not afraid of sharks or lobsters or jellyfish, but the whole dark world underneath—the droopy, slow-moving spiny fish, the eels, the currents and sinkholes—these things make her want to hurry back home, ride a heated subway car to the movies, where she can be absolutely sure of what will happen.

Bill had suggested the trip; he has nostalgic feelings about the place, about his childhood. He tells her it's where he feels most alive.

The snow is falling heavy on the ocean, dissolving into it, swirling on the front deck of the ferry. For a minute, Eleanor can hardly believe what she's seeing—the huge iron boat, painted blue, named for a governor; the gray water—a mile deep?—the big flakes of snow. She can't see anything in the distance.

Her enthusiasm for Manhattan goes up and down, but she's been feeling especially steeled for battle, feeling there is no other place she could live. She's in her third year of medical school, and while she spends most of her days exhausted and depressed, the occasional aortic anastomosis—cross and connect, like radiator hoses—amazes her; the resilience of the body calms her. She does not worship procedures in the same way some of her fellow students do, but a week earlier, when she first saw an open chest cavity, she forgot herself—and Bill—and thought only about her child, growing inside her. She saw a glimpse of the ribs, which have a plastic sheen, and she saw the turmoil inside this patient's body—a fatty heart, dark lungs—and she dreamed about the perfection of her child. Her most recent guess: he (she has decided the baby is male) will be a trombone player in his middle school band, and he'll be an actor, preferring musicals, and he'll eat cereal by the bowlful. She sees blond hair and skinny legs. It made her so wistful and worried, she nearly left the operating room.

And this as well: he will live a long life; he will watch Eleanor grow old and die, and he will have his own family, and perhaps a woodshop in his garage, and he will be fascinated by other things, by the habits of turtles, perhaps, or the geology of Antarctica.

Bill returns with a miniature bag of pretzels which he drops in her lap. "We'll find something when we arrive, sweetie," he says. Then he's back to reading the paper.

(At first Bill's laconic manner made her nervous; she liked

the muscles in his legs, and his dark eyes, but she wondered if he was smart enough. She realizes now that he is.)

They've been living apart because of Bill's job. He writes about food, and it's the *Globe* that gives him work. He's made a name for himself. He is unconventional and fickle. He gets a lot of hate mail. He fixates on one thing—the mushiness of the cauliflower marranca, for example—then drums his point to death. Eleanor finds his articles hilarious. She tries to visit him as much possible, which ends up being very rarely, but when she does they go out to dinner on the *Globe* and he writes about it. When Bill visits Eleanor in New York, she treats him to stories of pig vivisection, which is what she's been doing lately as part of her training. It's not what she expected: she had never seen a pig before, either. She was thinking slick and pink and round but these pigs have grayish black hair and are skinny—they look almost like cats.

When they're not together they talk on the phone at night. There's been a lot to talk about lately. She's easily discouraged. Who has a baby during medical school, and who in his right mind marries a pregnant medical student living four hours away? Bill is an optimist. He says they can do it all. She asked him, marriage? He said, Sure. Was that a proposal? They were on the phone and she told him, come on, let's do this correctly. If we're doing this over the phone, you should at least be kneeling.

"I'll wait until I see you," he said.

Bill sees things at face value. He has the enviable ability to recognize—in the most straightforward of ways—how much he loves her. She's supposed to be the literal-minded one, the scientist, the pragmatist, but Bill, he's a stickler for the truth. He has beliefs. She admires his intelligence, his memory, his ability to synthesize squirrelly ideas. His thoughts come choreographed, tightly outlined. Bill will teach the child how to tie a slip hitch, fold clothes, speak grammatically.

The ferry's route winds through a tight passage, and she's amazed there's enough depth to keep it from running aground. They're going much slower now, and they steam past a fluorescent green navigational marker—Bill calls it a can. There is an austere bird with a hooked beak nested on top, staring at the ferry through the snow.

"Eagle?" she asks.

"Osprey," he says.

"Are you sure?"

"Positive," he says. "They're everywhere up here. It's the Cuxabexis mascot."

"No chance it's an eagle? It looks like one."

"It does," he says. "But it's an osprey."

This is Bill at his best. She likes it when he doesn't back down. When they visit each other, they wrestle—they spar in bed, or on the living room floor—and he has learned not to let her win. In high school, his Cuxabexis basketball team traveled the state. He was the point guard and his dad was the coach. Bill uses some of his father's old expressions. Persistence pays. That's one. Another: Life is not fair. His father was a geometry teacher, too, and would bring a tape measure to the first practice every season, showing his team that the diameter of the basket is exactly twice the diameter of the ball. Bill tells this story with great pride; his father died a year ago, of a heart attack.

His father also insisted that bank shots, correctly calculated, are more accurate and much more satisfying than non-bank shots. Bill is a bank-shot man.

The ferry slip on Cuxabexis is made of long gray wooden planks nearly as tall as the boat itself. The nearby wharves are covered with tangles of frayed green nylon rope, rubber boots, and tubs of fish. The harbor is silent. The thick spruce forest comes right down to the shore, with gnarled trees growing on the rocks.

THEY STAY WITH BILL'S AUNT, FRAN—THE SISTER OF HIS dead father. She looks about sixty, with long hair and a steady chin. She has Bill's pretty eyes. She walks them to their room on the second floor, and she smiles at the poster bed with its pink pillows and red blankets. The remainder of the room is empty except for a plain wooden dresser topped by a bowl of heart-shaped soaps. The view is the neighbor's house, plastic stapled over the windows, aglow with green light.

"You two are a handsome couple," she says, and suddenly Eleanor is struck by Fran's beauty. She looks like an old film star. "We'd love to see you have some babies, Billy."

"In time," Eleanor says.

"Soon," says Bill—but Eleanor pinches his arm. She's not ready to talk about the baby with anyone.

"Well, it would make me happy," says Fran, giving them a smile. She is wearing a maroon cotton dress. Her stare is unfocused but kind. "This island has always been a good place for growing a family. Eleanor, I've raised ten children here. Maybe you should move back, Billy." She winks.

"We're just here for two nights," Eleanor says.

"That'll be long enough," says Fran.

Bill sits on the poster bed. "Big game tomorrow night—how's George playing?"

"He's on top of it," she says. "We're undefeated."

But meat is the issue most pressing to Eleanor. "Are there restaurants here?" she asks.

"You can eat with me, dear," says Fran. "We'll start at seven."

Then she leaves, and Eleanor closes and locks the door after her. She moves toward Bill on the bed. She unzips her jeans.

"Hi," says Bill. He lies on his back and she pins him. He puts his right hand on her left breast, over her shirt. She leans down and bites his neck, and he pulls her underwear down enough to get his fingers on her. He starts very slowly.

She tumbles over on her side, keeping a knee raised. She unbuttons the top three buttons of his shirt and reaches in to put a hand on his warm chest. She kisses him again and his face is concentrating.

When she comes, her legs close on his hand. She keeps it that way, her own hand gripping the back of his neck.

Bill had slept with six women before Eleanor, and she knows all of their names. They are no match for Eleanor. The first time she had sex with Bill—he was a senior in college and she had a research job at Mass General—was awful. He had her on her back, he didn't look her in the eyes, and he pumped like a piston drill. She didn't know quite how to take it; she thought, at first, he was being ironic, but then she realized he needed some guidance.

"That's quite something," she had said. He lived in a basement apartment, with windows near the ceiling.

"Really?" he said. He had a colorless imagination back then; he thought she was complimenting him.

You're an automaton, she thought.

She got him to slow down, relax, and she felt less lonely. Bill became her earnest student. They were at a Ukrainian restaurant in Watertown when she told him she loved him—the first time she had said such a thing—and when they woke up the next morning together, Eleanor's brain was unusually quiet.

FRAN'S KITCHEN HAS A LOW CEILING AND NONE OF THE hokey charm Eleanor expected—there's a TV next to the microwave, and empty boxes of sugar cereal stacked by the trash.

"Going to the pep rally?" asks Fran. She has changed out of her dress and is wearing purple sweatpants and a purple T-shirt. When she sets the bowls of soup on the table, her round biceps show under her loose skin.

"Definitely," says Bill.

"Everyone's going to love seeing you, Billy," she says. She sets bowls of soup in front of them. "George wants to play you sometime."

"Your grandson?" Eleanor asks.

"My son," says Fran.

"Oh," says Eleanor. "Excuse me." Bill has told her little about Fran—she was a relative he'd always liked, but he'd never spent much time with her as a kid.

"He's fourteen," she says. "A full six-four."

"Great news," says Bill.

"So, when's the wedding?" Fran asks. She blows on a spoonful of soup, then puts it in her mouth.

Bill says, "Well, we haven't—"

"Why not?" Fran asks. Her look is earnest; she seems genuinely concerned.

"We'll tell you when we're ready, Fran, I promise," says Bill.

"Okay, Billy," says Fran, smiling. Eleanor has just started her soup but Fran ladles her more.

Eating the soup has calmed Eleanor. She reaches under the table and feels for Bill's crotch. He swells in her hand. "I'm pregnant," says Eleanor.

Bill looks as though he swallowed wrong.

"That's wonderful! I could almost tell," says Fran, reaching across the table and squeezing Eleanor's arm.

"You're the first person we've told," says Eleanor.

"Your father would be so happy," says Fran.

"Yes," says Bill, and his face is flushed—he's happy. Eleanor knows exactly what he's thinking: My wacky girlfriend, so unpredictable.

Fran takes Bill's empty bowl to the stove and fills it. "You know, the rabbits that went into this soup—they're amazing," she says. "One of them gets born on a Monday, and by the middle of the following week, he's a granddaddy."

"That sounds kind of impossible," says Bill.

"I'm not sure on the math," says Fran. "Believe me, though, these bunnies are out of their minds."

The soup is delicate, plenty of bay leaves and marjoram, and the cubes of meat are lean but not dry.

"Have you ever seen rabbits do it?" Fran asks. "It's damn exciting. Not in a perverted way, either. It's just that they're efficient. Strenuous. It's really very inspiring."

Eleanor wonders if Bill is used to conversations like this with his family. "When do you watch them?" she asks. Bill is turning his soup spoon in the bowl, still flushed and smiling.

"Up at Gus Reed's farm. I walk up there sometimes. We'll go tomorrow. They have these little tiny penises—"

Bill laughs. "So what do you think of Cuxabexis, sweetie?"

"Great soup here," says Eleanor. Everything feels exciting: the trombone player in her uterus, Bill's family, being on an island where rabbits are fucking.

"You two do the dishes," says Fran. "I'll get my coat and we'll leave in ten minutes." Before going upstairs, she looks at Eleanor and smiles, puts her hand lightly on Eleanor's cheek and says, "You're very lovely."

THE PIGS SHE'S BEEN OPERATING ON IN SCHOOL: THEY MAKE her sad. All of the students wear gowns, gloves, and masks, but nothing is sterile, probably because they aren't concerned about fulminant sepsis in patients who will be euthanized at the end of the hour. She tells Bill that the worst thing about it is that she uses Nembutal, which works as an anesthetic but not a paralytic. That means when Eleanor grazes a nerve with her scalpel, the pig's muscles twitch. She's cutting him up, the little guy, and he's moving all around.

"But the pig is basically dead, right?" asks Bill.

"I guess so," she says. "He won't ever wake up." She gives him the Nembutal, intubates and hooks him up to a ventilator, then takes out a lung, or cross-connects blood vessels, whatever she's told.

"It's a pig, though, sweetie," says Bill. "Just a pig. Think about how much you're learning."

"You should see them," she says. "They're just so small and skinny, and they're on their sides, asleep. Dreaming of the old days."

"The old days?" asks Bill. "What?"

"You know, back with their mom, running around outside."

"Pigs don't remember like that. They don't dream."

"I bet they do."

THE SNOW HAS STOPPED AND THE CLOUDS ARE LIFTING, billowing together, dark bluish gray on the horizon, clearing patches of night sky. The road has already been plowed. The sidewalk, too, has been cleared; it's set above the road, in the side of the hill by the harbor, and Bill and Eleanor and Fran walk along it under pine boughs. Fran is dressed entirely in purple: purple boots, purple sweatpants, purple down coat, and purple bandanna around her head. There are no boats in the harbor, but the clean, sturdy wharves are well lit by high-set street-lamps, giving the path where they walk an orange hue. The wind is picking up, but Eleanor feels warm. In front of every house they pass, there is a neatly stacked pile of green-wire lob-ster traps, and symmetrical bouquets of fluorescent lobster buoys, tied together for safekeeping. All the vehicles they see are trucks, all of them high-gloss reds and blues and dark greens.

"See the flags?" Fran asks. Every wharf has a flagpole—

shorter than usual, bare wood bleached by the sun—and each one flies an American flag and two others.

"The blue one's Maine," Bill says to Eleanor. "The brown spot in the middle's a moose."

"We got our flag—it's that white one—before Maine was even a state," Fran says, proudly. "French pirates. They stock-piled firs here." Eleanor nods—she sees the pirate in Fran, and she's envious.

In town, they turn off the main street and walk up a steep hill past an old cemetery full of enormous, ornate tombstones and mausoleums. The wind is warm.

The further they get from the harbor, the warmer it gets, and by the time they reach the high school, Eleanor's face is flushed and her feet are sweating. It feels like a different sea-son. There are birds overhead—ospreys?—that are making their high-pitched calls, circling near the wide thatch nests they've built in the top branches of the spruce trees. Eleanor hears water running beneath the ice on the creek by the road.

Fran pounds three times on the side door. When it opens, a young girl peers out. She looks at Eleanor and Bill, her brow wrinkled. "Hey, Fran," says the girl.

"This is Billy," Fran says to the girl. "You're too young, dearie, to know who he is. He's a legend."

The gym is small, but the bleachers are packed—it must be the entire town, and many are dressed like Fran, in purple. They murmur. When the three of them get to the center of the bleachers, the crowd parts and they climb to the back row. A man in overalls in the third row winks at Fran, then smiles.

Everyone is staring at Bill. The back row makes room, and Bill and Eleanor sit on either side of Fran.

Eleanor has never seen anything like this. It feels like church. "Why is this pep rally closed to outsiders?"

"We've had people from the other islands come over, try to get our game plan," Fran says. Then she takes Eleanor's hand and says, "I'm so glad you're here."

The cheerleaders arrive first, and they are magnificent stock—tumblers, cartwheelers, smiling hard. They bounce on powerful legs, spring into pyramid formation.

"Go, Ospreys!" they scream, all strong shoulders and flat chests. Eleanor has always resented cheerleaders, but she loves these ones. They're doing their job, red-cheeked and loud.

Then, blasting from a side door, the team. CUXABEXIS on their chests, purple letters on brilliant white uniforms. They are all tall with lithe, pale muscles and crew cuts. They slam the ball against the hardwood in their sprint to the basket, and then—flash!—they're up by the rim and ever so gently laying the ball in the basket. The cheerleaders are feeding on it, jumping by the sidelines. Everyone's on their feet now, and the fight song kicks in:

> *Cuxabexis, Cuxabexis*
> *From the spruce trees on high!*
> *Cuxabexis, Cuxabexis*
> *Till the day that we die!*

"That's George, there, number twenty-four," shouts Fran, and Eleanor sees the resemblance. He has bright eyes and a high forehead—another pirate. As he waits in line to do his layup, he jogs in place. He has hairless, strong legs. When he gets the ball, his movements are hesitant, but he leaps up to the basket and slams the ball down.

"Wow," says Bill.

"His daddy can jump, too," she says, winking at Eleanor.

A middle-aged man with slicked-back gray hair, dressed in a tie and tweed jacket with blue jeans and farm boots, walks from the bleachers to the microphone at center court. He taps on it and it whines. The crowd silences. "Ladies and gentlemen, we have a special guest tonight. Many of you remember the '89 tournament, when our Ospreys torched Islesboro for ninety-nine points to win States. The point guard on that team, the son of Bill Haskel Sr., scored thirty-one to lead the team. He's come all the way from Boston today, and I hear he's got a happy lady with him, who's soon to be bringing us Bill the Third. Let's have one more *Cux, Cux* for Billy Thrill Haskel."

LATER, IN THE POSTER BED, ELEANOR'S ON TOP OF BILL. He's inside her. "Billy Thrill," she says. She is no longer mad the secret is out; after all, she is the one who told Fran, and Fran is a pirate. Bill is slow in his fucking. In the end she relaxes all her weight on him.

"Will you marry me?" he asks.

"What?"

"I'm asking in person," he says.

He gets out of bed and kneels on the wood floor, naked, wincing at first from the pressure it puts on his bad knee.

"Billy Thrill," says Eleanor. "Yes."

When he gets back into bed, they lie on their backs and Bill pulls the blankets up. She listens to their breathing for a while, then she says, "Let's get up early and walk around the island," but Bill is already sleeping.

THERE IS A KNOCKING AT THE DOOR. IT'S BARELY LIGHT. Eleanor looks at the digital bedside clock which reads 6:55.

"Hello?" she mumbles.

"Hey, it's George," says a voice behind the door. "Mom told me to get you guys up. She said you want to see the rabbits."

"Give us a few minutes, okay?" says Eleanor.

"No prob," he says.

Bill has slept through this exchange, but when Eleanor rubs his head and kisses his cheek his expression turns cross.

"Jesus," he says.

"Come on, time for a walk."

"Right," he says. "Go to it." He pulls the blankets over his head.

Eleanor gets up and spends a minute on her knees in the bathroom, gripping the sides of the toilet. She vomits. She brushes her teeth and puts a cold washcloth on the back of her neck. Eleanor sees that Bill has guilted himself out of bed and is putting on his pants. His hair is flat on his head and he yawns wide. His face is gray and his eyes are nearly shut and Eleanor tries to guess what he's thinking. She wonders if she should know, now that they're getting married.

For the walk, George is dressed in jeans and matching jean jacket. He wears huge untied purple sneakers and holds a worn leather basketball. Bill and Eleanor are on the sidewalk and George is in the road, walking in long strides, bouncing the ball, weaving it between his legs and behind his back. It's early but it's warm; there's a trickle of snowmelt between the road and the sidewalk. Fran is off running errands.

"I always keep a ball with me," says George, smiling. "For good luck, you know?"

He's a skinny giant who seems to take his life quite seriously. He's got the soft close-cropped hair of a baby starling, no whiskers at all, red cheeks. Eleanor can't imagine how his team wouldn't win their game; the island feels mysteriously pointed in that direction.

"George, you know what we're coming up on, around the corner," says Bill. George grins, staring down at his shoes. They're on a road with a long row of small white houses built close together under large bare oak trees, a post office, and a coin-op laundromat. Then, a basketball court comes into view. The air smells salty, and with the sun shining through the trees, the shadows are sharp.

Bill points to the court. "You ready, hotshot?"

"I probably shouldn't," says George, still smiling. "I've got a game tonight." But he's taking off his jeans, and he's wearing his uniform underneath.

"I'll take it easy," says Bill. "Just a friendly game. My knee's gimpy, anyway." Eleanor knows they'll both kill for a win: George wants to beat the legend, and Bill wants to prove he's still young.

"Where's the farm?" asks Eleanor.

"Just up the hill," says George. "You can't miss it."

Bill strips down to his T-shirt and tightens his sneakers. When they step on the court, he lets George have the ball first. Bill crouches in his defensive stance, no smile. Billy Thrill.

"I'll be back," says Eleanor, but neither responds.

She climbs the hill. A breeze comes through the spruce trees. By the side of the road, fiddleheads poke through the bramble. In the clearing at the top of the hill sits a modest white farmhouse with a wide wet lawn spotted with melting snow. There's a large pen up near the house with a low wire-mesh fence. An old man stoops in the pen with a bundle of hay in his arms. He has the ground nearly covered, sprinkling the hay here and there. When Eleanor gets close, she sees a huddle of white, black, and brown rabbits by the side of the barn, at the edge of the pen. There are perhaps thirty of them. They're not moving much; their heads are down, and they're nestled up close to each other.

"Hello, dear," says the man, looking over at Eleanor. His hands are bloody and he wears a darkened smock.

"Are they cold?" she asks.

"Not sure," he says. "They usually do this before I clean them. They must know."

"Can I help?" she asks.

He looks at Eleanor hard. Then he smiles. "I don't really need the help, but you could do the knots. My fingers are bad." He sprinkles the last of the hay and then holds his hands out to her, palms up. He has blood up to his elbows. "I've got a bit of a shake," he says, and he does, but his hands are huge and strong-looking. He opens the gate for her.

"Saw you at the rally last night, dear," he says. "So glad to hear you're bringing Billy back home. Hope I'll be around to watch Billy Three play."

She nods.

"Billy's a good kid," he says.

He walks slowly to the bundle of rabbits and picks out a white one by the scruff of its neck. He hands it to Eleanor.

"First we've got to tie its back legs," he says. "They don't like it much, but I can pop the neck straightaway and then they don't feel anything."

"Okay," she says.

In the barn, a rope is hanging from a roughly hewn rafter, leading down to a stool. She takes the rabbit's hind feet and cinches them with a square knot. The rabbit kicks and kicks. Then, as swiftly as promised, the man puts a thumb into the back of its neck and with his other hand pulls its head back. Then he cuts into it with a quick jerk of his knife. Blood streams to the hay. He skins it with one pull. The muscles are encased in a bluish, shiny membrane. She puts her hands around the slick, hot carcass. She's amazed.

"Yup," says the man. "That's all there is to it."

She thanks the man and says goodbye, looking once more at the beautiful huddle of rabbits, thinking again about her baby—wondering if she's ready to take care of something so helpless. She walks down the hill, past George and Bill, blood sticky on her hands, feeling excited. She loves Bill, but she can't talk to him now, she needs some time alone on this island. She watches George glide past him, leaping up to the basket and with one hand cramming the ball in the hoop. A question from Bill about the rabbits, about the blood on her hands, would depress her. *You helped Gus Reed kill his rabbits?* He would only be curious, but there are so many things she can't explain to him. He helped, but the baby is hers. In seven months she will be as big as a phone booth. She will ride the subway to the hospital to give birth. I'll be there with you, Bill has said, I will.

Okay, Bill, okay.

This baby is hers. She already loves it so much she could eat it—this is something else which Bill wouldn't understand. *I don't mean that literally*, she'd have to say. She keeps walking, all the way to the far side of the island, on a road without houses, the thick spruce forest coming right down to the edge of the road. The warm wind gives her chills.

When she reaches the ocean—a house on a small plot with open views to the east—she sees waves slamming the nearby shore, loud and dramatic. Beyond this, though, are miles and miles of water, a surface as smooth and shiny as the hood of a car. This calms her, for now, which is what she'd always hoped an ocean could do.

[FIGHTING AT NIGHT]

W<small>E LIVE ACCORDING TO AGREEMENTS, AND I HAD MADE</small>
one with a 220-pound brawler named Brick Chickisaw. It was
typical behavior for me. After getting a taste of something
good, I needed to gorge myself.

I'd seen him at the state fair up in the county, in Caribou. He
bloodied a Biddeford man—knocking him out in two minutes
thirty-three seconds—and afterwards, caught up in the excitement, I climbed through the ropes and approached him in the
ring. His trainer, a short man with a gray ponytail, stepped in
front of me. Brick was climbing off the other side of the canvas—
his massive shoulders caught up in the ropes. I asked the trainer
if they could come down to the coast for a fight in August.

"How much?" he asked.

"Five hundred," I told him.

"You got girls?" he asked.

"I can make arrangements," I said. We shook hands. "Point Allison, August second."

"I'll ask him," he said. "Five hundred, even with girls . . . it's not the greatest offer. We'll see."

"Eight-hundred," I said.

"Who's the fighter?" he asked.

I cocked my head to the side, then rolled my shoulders back. "Jason Chalmers."

His eyes were black. "He'll kill you, this guy. Did you see the fight?"

"I'll give you even odds I knock your man out," I said. "Any money, we'll take the bet."

"Sold." He had a grin like a submarine sandwich, greasy and soft.

Alice would be pleased—she was my coach and financier. Brick hadn't fought outside of Maine yet, but he was a pro fighter, the real thing—he hadn't lost.

ALICE WAS MY FRIEND PETER'S WIFE; THE THREE OF US lived together in a farmhouse with a pond on the Point Allison line. She'd learned about boxing as a girl—her father and her uncle had been Olympians, they'd fought for Canada in the fifties, so she knew the sport well. She saw my strengths and weaknesses, and trained me accordingly, pushing me to drill my footwork for many hours each day. She was small—she had slim boy's hips and thin legs—and her voice was quiet, but with a few sharp words or a changed expression she could level me, make me feel ashamed of my shortcomings. That was her gift as a coach. A week after I'd gone to Caribou, I was lying on the lawn after a workout and Alice was sitting next to me.

"You're crazy to box this guy," she said. "I've heard about him."

"What have you heard?" I asked.

"He'll never fall down," she said. "He's just one of those fighters—an oak. That's what my dad called them. Oaks."

"You haven't seen me in a real fight," I said.

"I don't need to," she said. "You don't care enough."

"I'm working on it," I said, and I was. There were days when I knew that being slow could get me killed. Those were days I could train and train and train, without rest, without sleep.

She lay down beside me and I was close to sleep—I'd jumped rope and run sprints for two hours. I stared at the clouds, then closed my eyes. She whispered, "Maybe Peter's cheating on me. He barely talks to me anymore."

"No," I said. "He doesn't. Not a chance."

"If he does, I'll kill him," she said.

"I'm sure you would," I said. "He knows that."

I dozed off, my sweaty legs sticking to the grass. When I woke, she was sitting up again. She said, "I've been thinking."

"Yeah?"

"You're way too slow on your feet," she said. I could imagine her, then, among the big boxing oaks in her family. "You're strong, but you're slow."

OUT THE BACK DOOR WAS AN OVERGROWN PATIO, A SHADED rock terrace set down in the ground like a root cellar. That's where Peter and Alice drank gin, and it's where I skipped rope and rattled the speed bag. I was atmosphere for them; they reclined and sipped from big glasses as I did push-ups or danced on the patio, flurrying combinations in the air. Peter egged me on, calling me names, and Alice timed and counted my reps—she kept everything in a blue notebook. I'd known them both since high school; they got married when we graduated, and I was Peter's best man.

She'd kissed me once, two months before their wedding, but I don't think she meant much by it. We were standing in her parents' kitchen, waiting for Peter to pick us up for a movie. She said she hated that I was alone. She said sometimes it's best not to think too much about your past, and she kissed me on the lips. It was quick and soft and after the quiet I told her I liked being alone, it was okay with me.

For my first training bout, I put on the red gloves— Ukrainian Thunderclaws—and crouched in the ready position. It was raining and misty outside, smelling of seaweed, but we were in the living room and Alice had stuffed the woodstove with maple and beech logs from the pile on the porch. The chimney pipe glowed orange. My head was floating from the heat, which Alice thought would make me tougher, and Peter and I stood facing each other, both swaying, knees bent, backs hunched, the puffy sixteen-ounce gloves hanging in front of us like balloons. Peter was a big Irish kid with thick red hair, a wide face, and a sturdy torso—he had a Rottweiler's build. I had him by about ten pounds, and I also had him on quickness and reach. It was in the fifties that night—June on the coast wasn't yet summer—but it must have been ninety in our living room. Alice watched from the couch in a bathing suit.

Alice's dog Tessa stood by the side of the couch. She was a

normal-looking spaniel except for her wide, meaty head. She barked and whined at Peter and me as we faced each other with our gloves up by our chins. "Bark all you want," I told her.

Then the periphery faded and I saw it clearly: punch Peter in the face as hard as possible, hurt him, make his eyes swell. There were times like this when I could really wipe everything away and listen to Alice's advice. If you take it easy on a run, you're dead. Lose concentration and you're dead. She said every minute—every second—of training presented me with a decision.

I was sweating from the stove and from dancing back and forth, side to side, trying to make him look slow; Peter's punches were strong but just off their mark. They were sliding off my face. I danced around him and he was swaying just a bit with those hulking arms and that red face, waiting for me to settle again, when again he'd send out a muscled jab, which again seemed to slip off my face.

Then there was a click in my brain and I set him down, floored him with one roundhouse Thunderclaw. Peter hit the carpet on his side, eyes open, and Tessa went to him and licked his neck. I shook my arms out, danced from foot to foot for a few seconds with him at my feet, then went to the kitchen and filled a frying pan under the tap. I brought it back and poured it over Peter's head. From the couch, Alice pushed him with her bare foot to make sure he was okay.

THIRTY STEPS OUT FROM THE PATIO WAS THE POND. I'D WAKE up in the morning and put on a towel, walk out in bare feet to swim. It was National Forest property—untouched—the kind of place where sounds stirred and hung in the air, amplified, and vision stayed bright and sharp. It was sunny most of the time, but when clouds came in, they came in quickly, rising in a steep stand on the horizon before coming across with thunder, lightning, and soaking rain. Otherwise, there wasn't a thing in the world that could bother you out there—we had this translucent peach-colored raft to float on, so you could lie on your back and be hypnotized by the sky. Finches and sparrows liked it by the pond, too; the overhanging tree boughs were full of them.

Usually we didn't wear bathing suits. It was no place for clothing, because it was far from the road and surrounded by ferns the size of umbrellas. The pond warmed in July to a perfect temperature, so that if you held still, you wouldn't feel the water against your skin. When I closed my eyes floating in the pond, I imagined myself dead and buried, quiet in the ground.

There were, of course, the realities of our jobs, but they didn't ask for much attention. Peter and I painted houses—Alice waited tables in town. More important was that we swam in the pond in the morning, then, after working, retired to the shade for refreshments. I drank a mix of fiddleheads, bananas, and fish livers. Alice and Peter stuck to gin, which they liked to drink late into the night, while I worked the heavy bag.

Peter was taking time off from painting houses, spending his weekends up north, in Baxter, fighting fires. He'd done it the past ten summers, since he'd finished high school. He trained the rookies. Late one evening, on the patio, he was having a drink and I was on the speed bag.

"We've got to have another spar soon," he said.

"Sure," I said.

"I've got some new moves," he said, sipping from his glass.

"I like that move you have, when you fall down, dead to the world," I said. "That's a great one."

"You got lucky last time," he said. "I was just about to come around." He poured himself another drink. Then he said, "I want you to keep an eye on Alice when I'm up in Baxter."

"Of course," I said.

"Just look out for her," he said.

"Right, I figured," I said. "I will."

Late afternoon the next day, he came out to the pond to say goodbye. Alice lay naked on a blanket by the pond; she was sleepy drunk, I was out on the raft. Peter lifted her sunglasses from her face and kissed her softly—first her forehead, then her shoulder. Her small thin lips didn't move, but she raised her hand toward him as he left.

I didn't envy them. I planned to live my life without serious attachments. I figured that was the way around pain, the kind I saw every day between them. Things had worked out fine enough for me alone.

ALICE'S PLAN TO RAISE MONEY WAS TO BUILD A RING ON THE back lawn and charge admission for my sparring matches. The town was full of men wanting to prove themselves, so finding opponents was easy. The guys living on the dump road, for example, were angry people. When they weren't hauling traps, they were killing deer or waiting for deer season, cleaning their guns. Alice scheduled bouts for me every Wednesday and Saturday.

The first to commit was Donny House. He wanted to brawl

right away, so we built the ring in three days, in the middle of the backyard. We made the frame from two-by-fours and the deck from plywood, under which we laid bags of sand so a falling body wouldn't break through. The ropes were ferry deck lines, supported in the corners by dock pilings dug four feet into the ground. Alice climbed the bordering spruce trees to clip the overhanging branches.

Donny hauled traps and was a proud athlete who wore his shirts and pants tight and spent money on his hair. For the spar, he wore padded headgear, filmy green shorts, and striped tube socks pulled up just below his knees. Alice was smart to land him as the first public bout; he was hated for his prissiness, and we knew people would pay to see him get uglied. That night, Donny was the only person in town who thought I'd lose.

The sky was a huge sheet of stars and the air was cool. Alice had rigged fluorescent lights in the pine branches above the ring. From my corner, I looked out and saw the small crowd which had gathered—thirty or so—some standing, some sitting on blankets in the grass. Alice climbed through the ropes with a placard reading ONE. She walked a quick lap around the ring in jeans, a light blue T-shirt, and a red baseball cap, getting whistles and applause.

Then she stepped down and rang the bell. I looked at Donny's headgear and went for his ribs, head down, frenzied, left, right, left, right, again and again, getting him to hunch over, curl into himself, unable to punch back. He backed out of it, though, and landed two good shots at my right ear. After the first round, I sat in my corner and Alice bent down to me and said, "What is this?"

"What?"

"You're nothing tonight," she said.

When she finished her lap with the TWO placard, she passed me without a look. As she climbed from the ring, she whispered behind me, "He'll kill you, this guy Chickisaw."

When the bell rang, I came at Donny House with an uppercut that took him off his feet. He landed on the plywood and Alice, after raising my arm in victory, helped him up and out of the ring.

THE NEXT MORNING, IN THE POND, ALICE HELD MY HEAD underwater. She said it was fundamental to my training.

"You'll hear your heart beating," she said, with her hand on top of my head, ready to press me down. Tessa swam in a tight circle around the two of us, breathing forcefully through her nose, her wet hair flat on her back. "Wait until you hear other things. You'll feel like your chest is going to explode, but that will pass. Don't come up until you like being down there."

When I was under, I opened my eyes and saw Tessa swimming, moving through the black water at an even pace, her legs pushing like a combine.

When I came up, my head was pounding; I yelled my breath in and out. I crawled up the bank and into the grass, collapsing. Tessa bounded out, ran to me, and licked my face. I tried to shove her away but my arms were useless. My eyes didn't work; I looked at the tree boughs above me, unable to focus on the birds.

"That was good," said Alice.

• • •

THE FIGHTS CAME QUICKLY. IT TOOK A FULL DAY AFTER
sparring to feel tip-top again—my headache would fade—but
Alice never let me rest much. If she sensed I was feeling good,
she'd take me out to the pond, or she'd tie bags of sand to my
ankles and wrists and she'd bike with me as I ran. I was ham-
mering the local competition, never allowing anyone past the
third round, but there was still a waiting list to get into my ring.
Red Heingartner was the only one to hit me hard—he had a
quick hook that snapped me back—but even with Red, all I
had to do was decide the fight was over, and it was over. A flurry
of punches and the man went down.

The move that felt best was a left-handed jab, which is
mostly just shoulder and arm. I'd have my right fist cocked
back—triggered—and as it twitched there like a promise I'd
come fast with my left.

Peter left for Baxter each Friday, returning Sunday. He
cheered me on at the Wednesday bouts, but he was gone on
Saturdays, and he knew he was going to miss the Brick
Chickisaw fight.

"At least they'll come for the beer, right?" said Peter.

"They'll come to watch me destroy the guy," I said.

We were on the patio. I had put my jump rope down, and he
was eating his dinner. He was quiet.

"I'll call in late that night from Baxter to see how it went,"
he said.

ALICE HAD STARTED TO ADVERTISE THE BIG FIGHT. ANYONE
who'd sparred with me would get in free; others had to pay ten
dollars, but admission included beer. Alice designed the poster,

which had neither a picture of me nor a picture of Brick. There were no boxing gloves or boxing ring, either. Instead it featured a full-length photo of Suzy Whitlatch, the girl Alice had hired to hold the placards for the fight. In the photo, Suzy was wearing a bikini, holding the card reading TEN.

"Suzy's an attractive girl," I said. I was skipping rope on the patio; Alice was holding a stopwatch.

"Pick up your pace," she said.

"That's a great bikini," I said. Is she for Brick?

"Keep your arms straight," she said.

"If I wasn't such a dedicated fighter, that's the kind of girl I'd like," I said.

"She's too young for you," said Alice. "And anyways, that's right. She's for Brick."

When I stopped, she held my wrist, counting my pulse, then entered a number in the notebook.

"We'll take the rest of this week off," she said.

THE NIGHT BEFORE THE FIGHT, I LAY IN BED LISTENING TO Tessa. Every few minutes she'd walk from one end of the front porch to the other, her claws clicking lightly against the slats. Alice slept down the hall, and she'd gone to bed hours earlier. At three, still awake, I got up and walked outside to the pond. I had heard the tree frogs from the house and I wanted to see them. I approached the pond quietly, taking slow steps, but when I pushed through the ferns, the frogs became silent. They swam at night; in the dark you could still see them, the whole pond a pattern of grays, their small wet heads bobbing above the surface. I waited there, standing still, until they started peeping again; first just one frog, then a few, then the entire crop. I started to cry, which surprised me. I thought to myself, this is the best I'll ever be. The strongest, the fastest, the most alive.

ALICE STARTED LETTING PEOPLE INTO OUR BACKYARD AT 7 P.M. She set up a card table near the ring where Suzy, cold in her bikini, poured beer into clear plastic cups. Alice was next to her with her arms folded, greeting people as they approached the table. I sat at a window in the living room, looking out at the gathering crowd, wearing a robe with the hood pulled over my head. I planned on staying there until Brick arrived.

Donny House was one of the first to come; his right cheek still had a bluish tint to it, but his hair was perfect, and he had brought his own chair, which he set up ringside. Red Heingartner, too, came early, and drank three glasses of beer within ten minutes of his arrival. I could tell his ribs hadn't healed by the way he laughed.

It had been sunny and clear all week, but clouds had rolled in that afternoon, a front from the south, moist air from offshore. In August, when fog came to Point Allison, it came for weeklong stretches. From the house, I couldn't see the pond, and I could just barely see the ring. I didn't see cars arriving, but people—lots of people—materialized through the mist, stepping up to the drinks table.

By eight, the backyard was full. Couples curled into each other on blankets; kids ran to and from the pond; old people sat in lawn chairs close to the ring. The rest of my sparring opponents had arrived, in various stages of recovery. Vince Civaglia, who ran Point Allison Hardware, was seated ringside, and was smiling and chatting loudly despite two black eyes and a splinted right arm. Another lobsterman, Ed Whitney, stood away from the ring, resting against a spruce tree with tape across his nose. I knew that in the years to come I'd see them around town and they'd say nothing of the training bouts. The Brick Chickisaw fight wouldn't be mentioned, either, unless I beat him.

When Alice turned on the fluorescent lights in the trees, the crowd cheered, and all the fog, from the house to the pond, glowed white. Soon everyone was clapping. At eight-thirty, Alice walked back to the house. When I saw her I opened the door.

"Okay, it's time," she said.

I knew the fight was set to begin in a few minutes, but when Alice said this, I was shocked.

"Let's go," I said, but I stayed where I was. It felt too early to walk out to the ring.

"Come on, now," she said. "Let's do it."

The thing was, I was ready to fight, but there was something else I was waiting for—some kind of indication that everything would turn out okay. Finally, I stepped out the door. As I did this, I felt a surprise was coming. It sounds crazy, but I half expected to vanish, or to fly up into the trees. I was waiting for it, whatever it was. When it didn't come I started walking slowly toward the ring.

"You okay?" she asked.

"I'm ready," I said.

"Let's go. Snap out of it," she said. "It's time."

"Alice, you've been a great coach," I said, but there was more I wanted to say. At my weakest I imagined I was in love with her, but the more I thought about it, the more I realized it wasn't that simple, and I had to keep my feelings to myself. At the very least I wanted to know if she really thought I could win. "What are my chances?" I asked.

"I think you've got one great fight in you," she said. "This could be it." She turned and headed for the bell.

I followed her, stepping through the crowd, then slipped under the bottom rope and into the ring. The cheering was loud. I stood in my corner, my hood pulled over my head.

Then I started shuffling my feet, sending out a right, a left, ducking, jumping back, lunging forward. The crowd responded to each move; they liked the combination flurries, the grand roundhouses, the flashing uppercuts.

I couldn't see Brick Chickisaw, but he was there somewhere, limbering up, getting ready to climb in the ring.

EIDERS

I SET THE DECOYS—MY FATHER CALLED THEM TOLLERS—
by dropping their small steel anchors overboard, paying out
line. They had thin keels on their underbellies that kept them
pointed in the same direction, looking exactly like any raft of
ducks you'd see up the cove. They were perfectly buoyant,
rigid. Some had their heads down as though they were feeding.

I'd been hunting with my father before, and while I liked
firing the gun and having the kick punch my shoulder, I never
aimed at the ducks. He assumed I was a lousy shot and tried
to improve my aim by telling me to relax, anticipate, breathe.

When I finished with the decoys I pulled the skiff ashore
and sat next to him. We were on a ledge in Jackson Cove, in
the dark. Fig stood on all fours next to us, shifting her paws on
the rocks, unable to find the right place.

"Christ, will you sit?" he said to her. I hugged her down to the seaweed. She was excited to hunt because it was the only time she could swim and hold dead birds in her mouth. My mother had never allowed it—she felt it poisoned the dog, turned her into something she wasn't.

The goal was to shoot birds for Thanksgiving lunch, but I wasn't sure I'd be eating with him—my mother had been pushing me to visit her in Boston. I was relieved and wanted to go, but at school we were having two-hour orchestra rehearsals to prepare for the Holiday Gala. Even at second clarinet, I had to be there every day. Missing even one day of rehearsal was out because my father believed rules were worth following—though it seemed the rules he especially liked were the ones which applied to other people.

The cold made my fingers slow and my insides weak. The overcast sky in the east was beginning to glow, but it was still dark on the reef.

"So, what about Melissa?" he asked.

"What about her?"

"It's pretty nice, isn't it? To be in love," he said.

"Who said love?" I asked, but he was right. I loved Melissa—I hadn't had a choice in the matter. She was this girl I'd met in the fall, during Family Skate at the rink, and it took me by surprise—she felt like a miracle to me. I was worried she'd find out I was ordinary. But she hadn't yet—she seemed to love me, too.

"You know, your dad can just tell with these things. I know you better than you think."

I stayed quiet on that one. I knew it was better not to challenge him when he was trying to be my buddy.

"You can be so cynical sometimes, Keith. I mean, come on. Admit it. She's a special girl to you," he said.

"What the fuck, Dad," I said.

"*What the fuck, Dad?* What the fuck? Jesus. Okay, listen," he said. Light from the moon brightened the far shore, so I looked over my shoulder. It had just slid out from behind the clouds in the west, above the trees, and it was full, with crisp edges. Dad scanned the water in front of us, not looking back at the moon. "Here's the thing," he continued. "You look at me like I'm an old man, which I am. I'm aware of that, that I look different than you. But what you don't understand is that I don't remember having ever gotten old. I still feel the same as you feel."

"Fine," I said.

"And I know what it's like to be your age. And to be in love. I apologize, but I do."

He'd dumped my mom—maybe she deserved it, maybe not. All I knew was that he came out looking like a coward. And a failure. This was not something I liked to think—it didn't make me feel any better—but it was the truth, and there's not much you can do about what's true.

He used a flashlight to load two red-cased shells in my over-under Beretta. The Purdy he used had automatic action, one barrel with adjustable choke; it held three shells. We knelt in the soft, cold seaweed in our plastic rain pants, ready to fire. The ducks sleeping in reeds up the cove would wake soon and fly to the ocean, and my father was quietly waiting for them. His face was dark gray and motionless. Fig sat in the seaweed, leaning into me; she was warm, but even better, she breathed quickly, excited and hopeful. She was nicely pressed against my side, knowing that once the guns roared, she'd be getting birds in her mouth. She helped me anticipate the sunrise; I could almost imagine the birds, too.

From the reef, my life seemed remote. I thought about orchestra, the hours I spent in rehearsal, how good it was when things sounded right, and how rarely they actually did. I didn't like many of the other people who played because they cared only about themselves and how brilliant they were at their instruments, but I stuck with it because it was something I could do without thinking. I played without worrying too much; at second clarinet, eyes weren't on me. In the past few weeks, we'd been working hard on some decent Tchaikovsky, "Elegy" from *Serenade for Strings*, which was actually beginning to sound okay.

"Wake up," my father said.

"I wasn't sleeping."

"Is your safety off?"

"I'm ready."

"Just don't close your eyes like that. They're about to come."

I heard a trawler steaming out of the harbor but saw only its red and green running lights. Soon, its wake reached us, the waves landing hard against the reef. This was something my father loved about the place, how raw and wild it was. The rocks were covered with barnacles, sea urchins, and thick kelp, and were exposed by the low tide for only two hours at a time. The water chopped when the wind and the current ran in opposite directions. From the reef, the cove opened up to the harbor, which opened up to the ocean; in the dark, I could see the red flashing light off Cuxabexis, and faintly, the white flasher on Matinicus Rock, nearly twenty miles away. Between me and the lights: a whole world. It made me want to hide, go back to bed, spend the rest of my life huddled away. Looking at those lights, with all the hugeness that lay between, my mind emptied and I shivered. And Melissa was what I kept coming back to; she gave me hope that I'd finally leave Maine, that I'd live a life that didn't closely resemble my father's, that I'd actually become a person of some interest—or perhaps that I was partway there. We'd already talked about getting married. The plan was to move to California eventually—maybe I'd keep on playing clarinet, or drive a cab. Melissa wanted to be a geologist.

At dawn, islands I'd known my whole life seemed altogether different, primitive. In the new light, just as I could see the outline of rocks on the far shore, it was like a clock had started—a distinct spray of eiders came up the cove. Fig hunched her shoulders as though she were trying to hide.

He whispered, "Ready," and fired twice before I had my gun up. I saw the cloud of birds through my shotgun's notch sight. After they passed, I pulled the trigger and the gun caught hard against my shoulder. My father was already up, looking out at his kills.

"Aha!" he yelled.

Fig bounded through the shallow water near the reef, then swam fiercely, her back well above the water.

Melissa had this laugh—louder than most, and I loved it because she was otherwise a loner. But when she laughed at something, it was like she was shouting—people paid attention, looked around to see who it was, and they'd see this shy, reclusive person. She was so confident that way. Her laugh was a strongly stated opinion, she didn't care what other people thought. I loved it. It made me ache, made me want to be the only person in the world she would talk to.

"Bull's-eye," he said. "Three are down." It was too much for Fig. She fetched the first, then dropped the first to get the second, but was unwilling to leave either. She circled around them, pumping her legs, breathing hard through her nose. The third wasn't dead; it thumped a wing against the water. She hadn't seen it yet.

I sat in the stern as my father rowed the skiff to get the hit ducks. As we got close, Fig picked one out of the water and brought it toward the boat. She held it softly in her mouth, and when I leaned over the gunwale to take the duck, she released it without a fight. She did the same with the second duck; both were large male eiders, black and white, birds you never see in summertime. I put them gently on their sides in the well of the skiff. They were warm and soft. Their wounds were small. We rowed to the hurt duck and Fig followed, and when she spotted the bird, the hair on her head bristled and her back came out of the water and she rushed to it. Fig was a strong dog with big shoulders.

The shot, dying bird attempted to dive—eiders are excellent swimmers—and Fig dove after it. I had never seen a dog go under, and while Fig's backside stayed afloat, the whole front half of her thrashed beneath the surface. The bird popped up ten yards away.

"Call the dog," my father said, standing unsteadily with his gun raised.

"Come on, girl," I yelled.

He opened the choke on his shotgun so as to widen the spray of pellets, not wanting to shred the bird, just finish it off. He fired.

Fig howled. After the pellets splashed the water, the bird stopped moving, and Fig swam to the skiff crying softly. She scratched the stern. My father reached down to help her, saying, "Jesus, is she hit?" I couldn't tell, and I moved to the bow to even out the weight as he pulled Fig into the stern. "Okay, girl, here we go," he said. My father had brown hair that hadn't yet gone gray, and he was tall with broad shoulders, but still, I was always surprised to see him do something which required a great deal of strength, like hauling Fig into the boat. He made it look easy.

Her neck was strained and she pawed at my father's chest. Seawater matted her hair, making her legs look skinny; she looked like a different animal, like a wolf or a coyote—her eyes had changed. He cradled her head in one arm and combed through the hair on her back and legs, looking for a wound. Fig shook in his arms. He raked carefully through her fur.

I rowed us back to the reef. My father took a wool blanket from his canvas rucksack and wrapped Fig. He carried her to the bed of seaweed where we'd fired our first shots.

"There's no wound. I think she's just scared and cold," he said, looking exhausted. "She didn't like being in the water when I fired. It happens with dogs. I'll hold on to her, keep her warm, keep her out of the water. You shoot for both of us and we'll be out of here in no time. Put a few shells in that Purdy. Maybe you've got the shot today."

I stood on the seaweed this time, unsteady in my boots. I kept one foot in front of the other and raised the shotgun to my shoulder. With one hand, I pulled my hat over my ears. My father and Fig sat a few feet away, both looking at me. Now that she was out of the water and away from the ducks, Fig didn't seem to remember what had happened.

The Purdy was bigger and heavier than my gun, and my limbs felt weak in my baggy rain gear. I pointed toward the cove. A mess of black ducks came silently up the gut and I aimed at the center, waiting. I watched with my hands on the cold stock of the gun. They passed.

"That's right, Keith," he said. "Choose your shot and be patient."

Another group of black ducks followed. It was a bigger group, faster. They came and went overhead. I kept my gun up, my eye in the sight.

"The kick isn't any different on that gun. Try to anticipate their line. Breathe out when you squeeze the trigger."

My knees were locked and my arms were tired but I couldn't move the gun from the sky. Eiders came and went. I aimed and followed their path in the sight. I decided to shoot but the trigger didn't go. My father stayed quiet.

Then came two groups of buffleheads, side by side, no single bird leading the way. I panned the barrel back and forth between them, but they flashed past. They were over the harbor when he spoke again.

"Should I take a crack at it, Keith? Why don't you sit down for a while. Fig's warm here."

"One more," I said.

I moved my elbows away from my body and raised the barrel higher. This time I saw the ducks well up the cove. As they got within range, Fig hunkered down again, lowering her head. There were at least fifty Eiders in the group.

"Holy Moses," he whispered.

I focused on the lead duck, whom I saw in sharp detail. Its neck was pointed straight, its wings snapped at a pace quicker than I could count. The rest flooded the sky, and then they were gone.

"Hell," he said, getting up. I kept the gun raised.

"Okay," I said. The gun was still pointed at the sky when my father took it from me, and my knees were stiff as I moved toward Fig, who looked up expectantly.

"Listen, Keith. What's this about?"

"What's what about?"

Then he started yelling, which seemed out of place in Jackson Cove—otherwise, it was completely deserted and silent. "Why do you waste my time like this?"

"I'm not," I said.

"You think I don't know that even when you shoot, you shoot at the goddamn clouds?"

"I'm a bad shot, Dad," I said. "Jesus, I'm sorry."

"You think I don't know you're shooting at the goddamn clouds every time we come out here?"

I stayed quiet.

"Don't pity me, Keith," he said. "I'll tell you something.

It's time for you to start being honest with me, good or bad. You owe that to me."

"Bullshit," I said. "I don't owe you."

"Is this about your mother?" he asked.

"No."

"Well, I don't know why else you'd hate me," he said.

"I don't hate you," I said.

Then, as though he hadn't heard me, he said, "It was a mistake."

"I don't think it was a mistake," I said. "I think we're all better off."

He turned away from me, toward the water. A wind was blowing steadily across the harbor, giving the waves white edges. "No. What I mean is, it was a mistake from the beginning," he said.

"Right." Now it was much more difficult to speak. "Okay."

"Are you listening?" he asked. "This isn't easy to say. I'm trying to tell you this. I wish things had been different, and I'm sorry for that, but it's as much your mother's fault as it is mine. It's no one's fault, really," he said. He turned back toward me. "Sit down. You're going to freeze to death."

I lay down beside Fig, holding her in both arms, breathing the smell of her wet hair and the damp wool of the blanket. Her nose was wet and her mouth was calm. She panted evenly. My father had said once that Fig was good company because she had no memory, and she didn't know she was going to die. I hugged her and rested my head on her back.

I watched my father as though he were on a stage. He got down on the reef to fire prone, on his stomach, his elbows propped up on a rock. He squinted and pressed his cheek against the stock. He faced the cove and didn't wait for the birds to get above us—he shot them head-on.

"Maybe you're right," he said. "Maybe I've forgotten what it's like to be your age."

The limit was six eiders and four blacks for each hunter; he had shot my quota and his, easily, emptying five boxes of shells, but he showed no sign of tiring. He loaded the Purdy again and again, popping the shells in place, snapping the gun closed. From one group of ducks he felled four with two shots, and as they fell to the water, he didn't move.

The birds came in intervals, every three or four minutes. I thought a lot had passed overhead while I had the gun, but they continued to fly in similar numbers from the cove. Where were they coming from? Were they circling around? I wanted them to figure it out. I wanted the birds who came up the gut, the ones who didn't get shot down, to report back to the ducks that were still sleeping in the reeds, way up the cove. *You'll all be dead*, I wanted them to know.

I walked across the seaweed to the skiff. "I'm going to start getting them," I said.

"Good," he said, without turning toward me. Then, quietly, he said, "Thanks."

Whitecaps had spread across the cove, making it hard to row, and hard to find the kills. I was surprised that the blackness of their bodies was easier to spot than the white shock of feathers some of them had on their sides. When I picked the first one out of the water, its beautiful neck was limp, and its body was almost entirely dry. I opened its sheer outer feathers,

144 ~ Officer Friendly and Other Stories

small and coarse, uncovering a wispy gray layer of down. It was a big eider, but it was light: its feet were shiny; its wings, which I stretched away from its body, were wide and sturdy. I couldn't imagine anything more perfect. I laid it in the well.

There were more than I expected. They filled much of the hull of the boat, enough so that I had to prop my feet on the aft thwart to keep from stepping on them as I rowed. Just when I thought I'd found the last, I spotted one more, a black duck ten yards away, and as I rowed toward it, my father fired the Purdy again, and another fell from the sky.

I drifted away from the reef but I could see it well. The tide had risen almost two feet since we'd arrived. I saw that my father was in the same spot, lying down but sloping slightly upward, with his arms propped on a rock.

The shot birds fell from the sky quickly—quicker, it seemed, than they could fly, which was hard to believe. And amid it all, my father looked more hopeful than ever. There wasn't much tide left—he'd be on the reef for only twenty minutes more—but he looked as though he had all the time in the world. Had Melissa been sitting beside me in the skiff, she might have thought we looked alike, my dad and I. I guess in some ways, from that distance, it was true: we could have been the same person. Only there's no way I could have hit half the ducks he was hitting, even if I'd tried. He was determined as hell. And he was a good shot, that's for sure. I wanted to know how someone comes to care so much about a simple thing, like shooting birds.

I drifted; waves slapped against the thin hull of the skiff, lower in the water now with the weight of all those stacked ducks. Wind from the north made my eyes water, but I could still see him lying there, waiting for another run of eiders from the cove. If the tide hadn't been flooding, I imagine he could have waited there forever. I would have waited with him. The gun finished the line that his body started, pointing to a spot just above the horizon.

[SEEING THE WORLD]

I WAS SEVENTEEN WHEN I MET JOHAN; HE WAS THIRTY-FIVE. We worked together in Portland at the Twilight Cineplex on Forest Avenue. I worked there because I had designs on being a movie director. I figured that any remote connection to the movie industry would further my cause—and in Maine, at seventeen, the Twilight was the best I could do.

To Johan, it was just a job, but he had other talents.

During his first shift—I'd worked there a month—I was wiping the glass top of the candy cabinet, and Johan stood next to me with his hands in his pockets, watching. We wore red bow ties with white ruffled shirts. He asked, "You like girls, Sam?"

"Sure," I said.

"Me, too," he said. "But you kind of hate them, too, don't you." He coughed out a fake-sounding laugh. He was tall, with a wispy mustache and messy blond hair. He had the kind of good looks best appreciated from a distance, or on film. Up close, his skin was cratered with acne scars, and his eyes were hazy.

"Sometimes," I said.

"Me, too," he said. Then he told me about his wife. He'd been married for three years to a woman in Bangor, but when she'd pressed him for a baby, he'd said no way. Then she tried to kill him.

"For real?" I asked.

"Rat poison," he said.

"Poison?"

"She put it in my coffee."

"Sounds like a good reason to move on," I said.

"You got a lady?" he asked.

"Nope," I said.

"You're lucky," he said, but I disagreed. It was tough for me to get dates, and I'm not sure why. I wanted to blame it on the fact that I lived at home with my mom, but the more likely reason was that I spent too much time with my video camera, monkeying around. By the time I met Johan, I'd already shot eighteen tapes of video—I was churning through batteries—flitting from project to project. For a while, I was dead set on documenting this rock-and-roll band, kids from my high school. I was convinced they were going to make it big and bring me with them. As it turned out, their trajectory was flatter than I thought. They played too infrequently and drank too much Jagermeister, so I junked the plan.

The first shot I took of Johan was this one: he sat on the

concrete steps outside his apartment building, smoking in his Cineplex uniform, with the clip-on bow tie hanging from his collar, unfastened. I filmed while I drove, with the window down. He squinted at the sun as he smoked. I clicked the power-zoom button and spoke into the microphone like a TV anchorman, "Johan waits for his ride, smoldering with regret."

While we worked, Johan had a lot of questions for me about women, and though I felt he was in a much better position to answer them himself, having been married, he disagreed, saying a fresh set of eyes could do him good. He liked to talk about sex. We shared stories in the quiet lobby while the movies were playing. Later, after the last showing, we'd lock the doors and run one of the movies again. We'd sit in the theater with at least one seat between us and Johan would shout at the actors on the screen. "Oh, please!" he'd yell. "Give me a break. That would never happen." I shortchanged him, for sure—I knew nothing about women—all my stories were fabricated. He never seemed to think I was lying, he just thought I was funny, the way I said things. Usually the conversations entertained me, but sometimes they made me feel pathetic for being so inexperienced. He could talk about one woman's body—the soft invisible hair on her upper lip, her smell, the way her hip bones felt, the exact topography of her breasts—for an entire shift. I videoed one of the conversations, and Johan went on and on, like a natural. That's when I knew Johan had the kind of jazz I was looking for, as a subject for a movie. He was like a combat soldier, a war hero—you could see it in his eyes. He was intimately acquainted with the battlefields of the heart. It was obvious.

"The best way to hook a woman is to make her hate you first," he said.

"You know it," I said, nodding.

"That way, you can only improve."

"Absolutely."

We'd been working together for a month when he knocked on the door to my house. Mom was a history teacher, so she had summers off. We were watching *Cool Hand Luke.* When I opened the door, there was Johan, holding an armful of clothes.

"The washing machine in my building's on the fritz. You don't mind, do you?"

I shrugged. He walked in. "Great place you've got here," he said, looking at the kitchen, then down the hall to where my mom sat in the living room. Johan gestured with his head—his arms were full—and yelled to my mom, "What's up?"

"Hello there," said Mom. In general, we had a great arrangement, my mother and I. She was very supportive of my dream to be a director, very accommodating of my artistic whims. In return, I cooked her meals, and cleaned the bathroom and the kitchen and took out the garbage. So when Johan finished his laundry and told us he'd been kicked out of his apartment, I had a short conference with Mom, telling her how important Johan would be to my career, and we made a place for him in our home.

"Temporary," said Mom.

"Of course," I said.

I knew this change would be tough on her. Mom was very

serious about her work, and about being a mother, and her style was so much different from Johan's. That's how she would have put it—*different.* Or maybe she'd say it was *interesting,* how he never did the dishes. She was reluctant to admit she was ten-times smarter than he was, and that it bothered her to have such a derelict under the same roof. Johan may not have been smart in the same way Mom was, but he was savvy. He was a go-getter. Also, he could be a real prick, and I figured I could learn something from him: how to be stubborn and selfish and single-minded and uncompromising. I needed these tools to be an artist—Mom wasn't setting a good example in that department.

That fall, Johan showed me an article from the *Press Herald* about the money people were making far down the coast, a few hours from the Canadian boarder, scuba diving for sea urchins. I was sweeping trash out from under the seats, after the late show.

"Ladies love fishermen," he said.

"That's right," I said. "Hold your thoughts for a minute." I ran out to my car to get the camera. When I returned, he said, "Think about it, how cool that would be—us making money as fishermen."

I aimed the camera, framing Johan in close-up. "We're rolling," I said.

"We'd wear the orange rain jackets," he said.

"Tell me about the article," I said. I panned back, then moved around him in a circle, my most dexterous camera trick.

"Seventy dollars a pound," he said. "They sell the eggs to Japan for seventy dollars! You see, the Japs—"

"Look at the camera," I said.

"—they kill for these eggs. And the sea urchins, they're everywhere. They say the bottom of the ocean down the coast—shit, what did they call it?" he said, flipping the page of the paper, scanning the article, wrinkling his brow. "Here. 'A big green carpet,'" he said.

I hit the auto focus, brought the camera to my hip. While it continued to roll, I snatched the newspaper from his hand.

The prospect of doing something real appealed to me; I knew it would broaden my range as a filmmaker. I'd lived in Maine all my life, and had traveled down the coast only once, to drive up Mount Cadillac. Mom resisted the plan. She'd been tolerant of Johan to a point, letting him grow marijuana on the windowsills in the kitchen and ignoring that he brought his girlfriends home late at night, but the idea of scuba diving in the wintertime, fumbling around in boats, jockeying for territory with career fishermen far down the coast—well, Mom didn't like the plan. School had started, so she was back at work, and she was unhappy I hadn't enrolled at the U. We were having breakfast—I'd gotten up at six to make her eggs and hash—and she said, "I have to say, Sam, my vote is a strong no."

"But you understand, don't you?" I asked. "This is something I have to do, for my movies."

"Jesus, Sam. How would catching sea urchins help with anything?" she asked. She wore small silver hoop earrings and an orange scarf and was shuffling through papers, not even looking me in the eye. "What about your job at the Twilight?"

"I need to *do* something, Mom," I said.

"There's always film school," she said.

"I want to be in the trenches," I said.

"That's exactly where that kid's going to put you, Sam." Then she whispered, even though Johan was fast asleep. "He's a jackass. You know that, Sam."

I was livid. "First of all, he's not a kid," I said. "And second of all, you think Rosenberg would have made *Cool Hand Luke* if his mom had kept him at home, locked up like a prisoner?"

"It's not that great of a movie," said Mom. I liked this about her. To her, taste was important. She had a bit of a bohemian streak, so her approach with me had always been hands off. She would argue with me, but she always allowed me to make my own mistakes—if I insisted on making them.

"But you get my point," I said.

She was quiet, and she shook her head. "No. But yes, I suppose in some ways I do."

"I need to meet other people," I said.

"If it gets bad, I want you to come back," she said.

"Definitely," I said, but I wanted to get a good taste of what was out there, so I didn't expect to return for a long while.

IN THE BEGINNING EVERYTHING FLOWED AS PLANNED. I PUT my camera and a box of videocassettes in the car along with a suitcase filled with memorabilia and warm clothes. We headed to Point Allison, four hours from Portland on the slow coastal route. I was anxious to get it all on tape. Johan drove, and I shot video out the passenger window. The colors of the beech and maple trees looked like fire through my viewfinder. We stopped for hot dogs in Bath, where we sat at a picnic table on the Kennebec River near the ironworks. Thick white clouds covered the sky. Johan said, "My wife was in love with being in love, you know? You got to watch out for that, Sam."

"I've seen it a hundred times," I said.

The blueberry fields we passed in Ellsworth were a mile wide, sweeping down to the ocean, spotted with white granite boulders. I made sure to say things into the microphone I might forget later about the footage—about smells, faint sounds that couldn't be detected, or feelings I had. I used the telephone poles flitting by to pace my narration, like a metronome. *From the car window, Sam smells burning brush piles, low tide, and dust.*

When we came to the end of the peninsula, it began to rain, so I pulled the camera inside and rolled up the window. We stopped at a gas station in the center of town. A young boy wearing a full suit of yellow rain gear pumped our gas. The saltbox houses along the main road were missing clapboards, and their lawns were unmowed. The market across from the gas station had plywood covering its windows; up the hill, there was an unlit diner, without any cars in the lot. At the edge of the harbor, a long row of tarp-covered boats sat in wooden cradles, resting for the winter.

The boy came to the window. Johan put his hand out to me for money, and I obliged. Then he asked the boy, "Where are all the summer homes?"

"Who you looking for?" asked the boy.

"No one," said Johan. "There must be some nice houses out there, on the shore. We're just touring."

Before answering, the boy squinted at us for a few seconds. "Take Spruce Head Drive, up there on the left, if that's what you want."

As we pulled away from the gas station, I got a tight shot of Johan. He stared straight ahead while the wiper blades slapped the rain.

"Cut the shit," he said, so I put the camera down.

We drove to the end of a dirt road, past a long stretch of dense spruce forest, to a two-story cedar-shingled cottage on the back shore. It sat right on the edge of the rocks, with steel pillars keeping it from tumbling into the ocean. Johan said, "This looks good."

"You know these people?" I asked.

"This place is shut down for the winter. We can camp here until we find a real place to live," he said.

He gave me a boost to the wooden rain gutter. I pulled myself up to the eaves, then scooted my way around the house, careful not to slip on the wet shingles, checking each of the second-story windows. I was soaked and cold. I could hear the low rumble of the surf against the rocks, but the rain against the roof and the gutter was louder. All the windows were locked. I got back to where I'd climbed up, then looked for Johan to tell him the bad news. He was standing in the driveway holding a large black stone, which he cocked back like a baseball and threw past me. It smashed the last window I'd checked.

"There you go," he shouted.

It was even colder inside the house, and damp, but it was carpeted everywhere, even in the wide stairwells. Downstairs, there was a twelve-foot plate-glass window looking out at the bay. We moved the couches aside, brought mattresses from two beds upstairs, set them up by the fireplace. The branches we collected from the woods were too damp to start a fire so we used a coffee table from the living room. Johan stepped on top of it, splitting it in half. He snapped off the legs, placed them gingerly on the crumpled newspaper in the fireplace, and once it was going, we topped the fire with spruce branches, which smoked and burned loudly. I set my clothes out to dry. We didn't turn on any lights in the house, so we went to sleep as soon as it got dark. I was dead tired.

My dreams were explosive that night—bright and real. I was walking alone on Forest Avenue in Portland—there wasn't anyone else on the street—then some kind of beast started chasing me, breathing loudly and snapping its teeth. I woke screaming, and Johan asked, "Jesus, are you on fire?"

I turned to the fireplace and saw only faint coals.

"You must have been having a bad dream," he said. "Christ. Keep it to yourself, will you?"

"Okay," I said, happy to be alive. I didn't want to explain that it hadn't been my fault—there'd been something chasing me.

The next day we went to Brother's fish house—Brother's Seafood of Point Allison—a dank unlit place with slush ice spilling off conveyor belts and the fertile smell of cleaned fish. The belts were running at a steady clip with nothing on them. In the far corner, a young woman wearing a T-shirt and rain pants was slapping a small squid against the concrete floor. Johan whispered to me, "Look at this one." I switched my camera on, starting with a shot of the wide fish house doors, open to the harbor. A front had passed through, so it was clear and windy, making the water light blue with whitecaps. The woman looked up at us as we walked in, holding the squid by the fleshy crests near its eyes. I zoomed in close. Her red hair was cut short like a boy's. I panned down to her arms, which were covered with a reddish brown film. She walked across the fish house to us with the squid in her hands.

She said, "You taking pictures in here?" She had a square, masculine chin but her eyes were softer—her eyelashes were long, and her eyebrows were delicate, and the smear of squid guts on her cheek didn't make her look dirty. If it had been a birthmark, it wouldn't have disrupted her good looks. When she got close, I saw how strong her arms and shoulders were— she was about my height, perhaps roughly my weight, but if we'd been wrestlers, she could have easily muscled me to the floor of the fish house in no time at all. I felt immediately ashamed by how little physical labor I'd done in my lifetime.

"We're looking for a place to sell sea urchins," said Johan, extending his hand to her.

The woman kept her hands on the squid. She laughed. "You read that article in the paper," she said. I was shooting close enough that her blue eyes and freckled cheeks filled my viewfinder. "She smells like rotten herring," I whispered to the microphone.

"Easy," she said, putting a hand in front of my lens. I stepped back, turning off the camera.

"Do you buy them?" Johan asked.

158 ~ Officer Friendly and Other Stories

"We're closed now," she said.

"Can you give us some advice?"

"You don't know Point Allison too well, do you," said the woman. She wiped her forehead with her arm, leaving another red smudge.

"We just need a place to sell the ones we catch," said Johan.

"Let me tell you a secret," she whispered. "They're not tough to 'catch.'" Then she heaved the squid toward Johan, shouting "Boo!"

Johan covered his head and leapt back.

She laughed. "You ever been on the water? Come on. What are you really here for? What's with that movie camera?" she asked.

"We just want to make some money," said Johan.

"You know how to dive?"

"That's what Sam's here for."

"Sam," she said, looking at me. I looked away; her eyes were too shrewd. "You know how to dive?"

"No," I said.

"You have a boat?" she asked.

"We're looking for one," said Johan.

"Bring your urchins here when you get them. We'll buy. If I'm not here, you sell them to my father," she said. She walked back to the conveyor belt, knelt down, and went back to work on the squid.

That afternoon, Johan and I were warming by the fire—he was telling me about a hooker he'd known in Lewiston—when we heard a pounding on the door. I crawled across the carpet, along the wall, and peeked out one of the porch windows. It was the woman from the fish house. I sat there for a minute, just looking. When she pounded again, I crawled back to tell Johan. He asked if I was sure it was her, and I said yes. We answered the door together.

"How did you know we were here?" he asked.

Her pickup truck was running. She wore a wool coat and blue jeans and gripped a white plastic grocery bag. "It's the kind of thing that gets found out pretty easily in a town like this," she said.

"You think it's okay if we stay here?" I asked. I caught her fish smell again, which made me want to get my camera.

"I haven't told the cops, if that's what you're asking," she said. "No one likes the people who come here in the summer, so you might be okay."

"You want to come inside?" asked Johan.

"I'm going home. I just wanted to tell you I'll dive for you if you put up the money, get me some new gear. We can use my boat."

"Bingo," said Johan.

"I'll give you twenty percent, tops." She handed me the plastic bag. "There's some dinner."

"Hey, beautiful, what's your name?" asked Johan, propping his hands on his hips.

"Listen, asshole," she said. "We can be business partners. I need a couple of lifters, that's all. And you need a diver." Then she turned and walked out to her truck.

"And your name?" asked Johan.

"Jane," she said.

"Good night, Jane," said Johan.

The bag contained two squid. I brought a shovelful of embers from the fire to the granite boulders just below the high-tide mark. I propped a rock under the lens of the camera and filmed as I cut the tentacles into strips and wrapped them around green spruce branches, toasting them over the coals. After we ate, we built the fire up, lay back on the flat rocks, and looked up at the sky, bright with stars.

"That girl wants to bed me," said Johan.

"She does?" I asked. The idea of it made my stomach tense—it unnerved me that I had been totally unaware of the romance brewing between them. It made me wonder if there was a frequency of sexual tension which I couldn't dial into—it was outside my range. Or maybe Johan was simply overconfident. That unnerved me, too. I had never been able to muster such bravado.

"Of all people, you should recognize the look she was giving me, Sam," he said.

"You're right," I said. "I guess I did see a little something."

We sold my car to a mechanic at Point Allison Auto for eight hundred dollars, roughly half what I'd expected, but it was enough to get the gear for Jane. It's not as though I didn't know he was using me to fund our venture—after all, the car that had been mine, which I'd bought with money I'd earned at the Twilight, was now being driven by a stranger. It's just that I was willing to compromise. We'd come all this way, we had a decent place to sleep, and if I returned home, I would have had to eat crow by telling my mom I'd failed.

We started urchining right away. The skiff had a twenty

horse power Evinrude on its stern, and as we motored out of
the harbor, I got some great footage of Jane with spruce-tufted
islands in the background. When I looked out at the open
ocean, I couldn't help but be overwhelmed by its seriousness,
its incredible depth and expanse—looking out to where the
earth curved was like trying to imagine the rest of your life, all
that remains unknown. But for Jane—I'd get her profile in the
foreground of my seascape shots—it seemed as though being
on the water was like sitting in the living room. She never
looked bored, but she was perfectly at ease. When we reached
the bigger swells outside the harbor, water sprayed over the
gunwale and I tucked my camera in the lazaret, a compartment
near the stern. I helped her squeeze her hands into thick neoprene gloves—two on each hand—so the urchin spines
wouldn't get her. She wore knee pads, so she could kneel on
the urchins, too. When she slipped the hood over her head and
zipped the front of the wet suit, she looked like a seal.

"You wear that well," I said, but she just furrowed her
brow.

We anchored off the north shore of Hay Island. Jane hefted
the iron weight belt around her waist and then slung two
tanks on her back. She took the end of a long loop of thick
nylon line down with her; in the boat, I held the other end. We
tied mesh bags to the loop, spacing them five feet apart. She
tugged on the line when she filled a bag. The water was
churned brown from the recent rains; we pulled up a new bag
fat with urchins every few minutes. We filled the skiff in two
hours. Her face was blanched and her lips were purple when
she surfaced. Johan and I each grabbed an arm and pulled her

into the boat. I gave her my parka, which she put on over her wet suit, but she couldn't talk yet, she was too cold. We motored our haul—ten fish tubs brimming with urchins, glossy and moving, like wet grass—back to Point Allison, dumping them in a holding pen in the middle of the harbor. Jane said we'd keep them there until the price went up far enough, then we'd get Brother to fly them to Osaka.

We drove with Jane back to her house, the three of us packed in the cab of her truck with the heat at full bore. When we got to her house—a tiny place, one-story, just across from the post office—Johan seemed surprised she wasn't driving us home. "Oh, no problem, we'll walk from here."

"Yeah," she said.

"You've got to warm up," said Johan.

"Yeah," she said. She was still shaking, and I could tell it pained her to seem less tough than usual.

"I could help you warm up," said Johan.

"Johan," she said, smiling, "my head's frozen, but I still know you're a loser."

"I mean, I could start a fire for you," he said. He was smiling, too.

"Eat some soup," I said.

"I'll manage fine," she said, opening the truck door and stepping out.

"You live alone?" asked Johan.

"Me and my guns," she said. She was being playful, but she wasn't wasting much time in getting from the truck to her house.

"You'll be okay?" he asked.

"You two should just run along," she said, flicking her fingers in the direction of Spruce Head Drive.

"I just want to make sure you're not sick," he said. "You look really cold."

"Just wait until January," she said, raising her chin to us as she opened the front door of her house. She stepped inside and closed the door without saying goodbye.

I asked Johan, "Can you translate for me?"

"Are you joking?"

"No," I said.

"You don't see it?" he asked. He was in a good mood.

"Not totally," I said.

"It's the dance, bro," he said. "God, I love the dance."

Even though I'm sure it was better firsthand, I was thrilled to be watching the dance up close. Johan had told me plenty of stories, but now I was getting to see him in action.

We'd been working for a few weeks when Jane suggested only one of us needed to unload the bags of urchins—we'd be better off using two divers. She started to train me. Her old wet suit fit me perfectly, and she had extra tanks, too. We began in the shallows at the far end of the harbor, in the estuary. We clambered down to the water through the reeds in all our gear. I had trouble breathing at first; as soon as I went under, I hyperventilated. Jane calmed me by resting a hand on my shoulder and explaining that she'd been the same way, at first. I didn't believe it, but I appreciated her efforts to make me feel more at ease—the efforts themselves made me calm down.

She gave me lessons at dawn, so they wouldn't interfere

with our urchining. Jane made sure I knew to exhale when I surfaced, and we eased into deeper water, away from the estuary, where the ocean bottom changed from mud to barnacled granite, and I saw hermit crabs and starfish and skate, all magnified through my mask. We'd flash hand signals at each other to communicate—thumbs up meant we'd surface, and she'd pat her buoyancy compensator if she thought I needed to inflate mine. But my favorite gesture was thumb and pointer finger making a circle, the other fingers raised—the okay signal—which we flashed each other many times throughout each dive. It was something I needed to do to stay comfortable. I'd flash her an okay and get an okay back from her, immediately. She was so straight-faced most of the time, so inscrutable, but these exchanges made me feel like we were really looking out for each other.

At night, Jane started visiting the house where Johan and I were staying, at first just to bring us firewood, which we paid her for (I paid her for). Little by little, though, her visits lengthened; often she'd stay for dinner, which was usually hot dogs we'd roast over the fire. I watched Johan and Jane closely, wanting to see what she saw in him. I knew she thought he was selfish and lazy and lecherous, but I also came to see she liked the challenge he presented: he was extremely confident in everything he did, and seemingly unwilling to change. Perhaps she wanted to change him; she was tough that way. But it might just have been that she was lonely, and that she liked how much attention he gave her. After one of our shorter workdays—the swells had been too high for us to work very long; we couldn't keep the boat from slamming

against the Hay Island reefs—we all went back to the house
for an afternoon snack of baby crabs. This was something Jane
had introduced us to: they were easy to find under rocks at
low tide. The smaller the crab the better it tasted. With an
oven mitt, I'd hold a frying pan with melted butter over the
fire; when we'd toss them in, the crabs danced in the brown-
ing butter before they turned red. Then we'd pop them in our
mouths, whole, washing the mess down with beer.

"I'm glad I'm not in their shoes," said Johan, nodding
toward the crabs.

"Don't be a pussy," said Jane. "They taste good, right?
Besides, they're tougher than you think. They don't need
shoes." She said this flirtatiously, which made me think she
might have been a little drunk—she'd had four beers. Her
cheeks were a bit brighter than usual. I thought about the two
of us underwater, how quiet it was.

"Imagine what that's like, getting cooked alive," said
Johan.

Jane laughed. "Well, I'll be fucked. You really care about
those little brainless things? What about all the urchins we
kill every day?"

"That's different," said Johan, popping a crab in his mouth,
crunching it without hesitation. "They don't have eyes." He
seemed almost sad.

"My stance is to just not think about it," she said. "Fuck the
crabs. Look out for yourself."

"That's usually pretty easy for him," I said to Jane. Perhaps
I was a little drunk, too.

"Yes, it is," he said, smiling, and I knew I'd been busted.

He'd caught me siding with Jane, trying to make him look bad, and he'd probably also seen me staring at her with curious eyes.

Jane slept over that night, on a third mattress Johan brought down from upstairs. It seemed he wasn't going to rush things. He let her sleep on his mattress by the fire, while he slept in the colder part of the room by the windows. It felt like a chess move; she was two feet away from me, but Johan had no reason to feel jealous—he just wanted to show me that even though I liked her, I didn't have the balls to make a move.

The next day was my first as an urchin diver. The water was much different than it had been during training; outside the harbor, the currents were stronger, and the visibility was muddied by sediment and algae. As Jane and I descended, a school of minnows shifted direction all at once, and the sun reflected off each of their little bodies like a burst of sparks. The ocean floor was just as the newspaper reported: carpeted with urchins, a bed of nails. When Johan tugged on the loop of bags to tell us the boat was full, Jane waved me over to her. I gave her the okay sign, and she flashed it back to me. I put my hand on her arm, but it's difficult to express anything when you've got a mask on your face and a regulator in your mouth, so I gave her another okay. She okayed me back, then pointed at one of the rocks we'd picked clean. She reached down and tugged at it, trying to turn it over, so I helped her, and when we flipped it, we exposed two lobsters with their claws flared. She grabbed them by their midsections, one in each hand, and put them in one of the bags on the loop. This was illegal, I knew, but how would anyone find out? I spotted another lobster crawling backwards away from us and, using her technique, took hold of it and put it in the bag with the other two. Then she gave me the thumbs-up sign, and we surfaced.

That night, we cashed in, towing the holding pen full of urchins to Brother's. Johan and I came away with nine hundred each.

Jane cooked the lobsters for us at her place, on the woodstove in the middle of the living room, which generated enough heat to keep us all in T-shirts. It was a welcome change from the house where we'd been camping. When she brought the lobsters to the table, red and steaming on white paper plates, their brown cooked eyes staring up at me triggered the thought: my camera had been in the lazaret for weeks.

Johan stepped from the bathroom, where he'd taken a shower and was combing his hair. "You okay, Sammy?" asked Johan. "You look like death."

"I'm fine," I said, but I wasn't. The last shot I'd taken was of Jane, on our first day of urchining. I'd been too busy learning how to dive and watching Johan's seduction to remember what it was I'd set out to do.

Johan slept in her bedroom, as I expected, and I slept on the couch. I tried to be as inconspicuous as possible—but the place was too small. They knew I was listening.

I crept out of the house before dawn and walked down to the town landing where we kept Jane's boat. I fetched my camera from the lazaret, feeling for it in the dark. When I got back to the main road, I waited on the shoulder with my thumb out for only fifteen minutes before a truck—loaded with the urchins we'd hauled, heading southbound—gave me my first ride of the day. I was in Portland by nightfall.

When he woke up, seeing me gone, I'm sure Johan thought I'd left so I didn't have to watch them fall in love. Maybe he was partly right. But what he didn't know is that I couldn't be a doer *and* a watcher. I had to split, that much was clear. Maybe there was still a movie there, in all that mess—I had to wait and see.

[PUCKHEADS]

WE'D BEEN HOCKEY PLAYERS, BUT WHEN DANIEL KOVACH and I got dumped from the team, forced by the headmaster to join the Drama Club, we made the best of it. We tried to remember how much we hated the screaming parents who attended our games, shaking gallon milk jugs with rocks in them, and the headaches our helmets gave us, and the absence of cheerleaders at our school. (Up the river, St. Dominic's had cheerleaders, dressed for the cold in woolen tights.) We worked hard to adjust. We missed the glory, of course—making the Channel Six sports highlights, or on game day, wearing our jerseys to class—but we convinced ourselves we were ready for a change.

It was a private school, North Allison Academy, an old brick building with a golden cupola and a front lawn riddled with crabgrass, and there'd been a time, when Kovach and I were freshmen, throwing a football on the lawn during study hall, when a moose had come out of the woods and walked right between us, without even glancing our way, continued clear around the school and onto the soccer field in the middle of a game. The headmaster—suspecting the moose's brain had been touched by viral infection—sprinted from the main building holding a rifle across his chest like a marine, and he took the poor beast down in front of everyone.

We tried very hard to be proud of our school.

Some of the students came from as far away as Portland, but I don't know why. There was an attraction to the school that didn't make much sense to me. My father was a geometry teacher—Kovach's mom taught art—so we'd been there, on campus, all our lives. We saw the school for what it was: a place where mediocre minds gathered to blunder along, a place where students were encouraged to do things boldly, in lieu of doing things well. Our library was full of unread books, and our pep-rally bonfires were always two stories tall, loud and blinding, unwieldy and hard to put out. It was broadly suspected that the public school in town offered a far better education.

Kovach had played goalie. The away games were hard on him. Picture St. Dominic's Academy, in Bangor; picture their cinder-block rink, with that vague smell of raccoon urine, and picture the mob of white-faced fans, standing behind Kovach in the bleachers, shaking those milk jugs. They were especially tough on him because he was good, and because he had a temper. They knew this.

They'd seen him, year after year—we were seniors.

Late January, in the rink at St. Dom's—we were down, 2–1—the fans were really laying into him, clapping and chanting and stomping, in unison, "KOVACH FUCKS HIS MOM!" (clap), "KOVACH FUCKS HIS MOM!" (stomp), "KOVACH FUCKS HIS MOM!" (clap). When I was off ice, I watched him from the bench. Usually, with the puck up at the other end, he'd skate back and forth in front of the net, slapping his stick against the goalposts. But with that chant filling the rink, he was just standing there, unmoving, crouched and waiting. Next shift, before the face-off, I skated out to him. The fans booed, then started in with, "MIDGET OR A DWARF!" (stomp), "MIDGET OR A DWARF!" (clap), "MIDGET OR A DWARF!" (stomp). The jeers were aimed at me: I was small.

"Okay," I said to Kovach. "Now take it easy." I smacked the side of his helmet with my glove.

He stared straight ahead, blank expression, so I tapped his pads with my stick, told him again to chill out, and skated back to the neutral zone.

On the power play, one of the Dom's kids streaked up the left boards, took a slap shot from twenty-five feet. Kovach flashed his glove up and caught it. The whistle blew. Kovach stood up from his crouch, calmly removed his glove, took the puck in his sweaty hand, then turned and gunned it into the stands, hitting a black-haired boy in the forehead, knocking him back. He fell from the top row of the bleachers. The benches emptied. Kids clambered over the Plexiglas. The St. Dom's scorekeeper—a man my father's age—jumped on my back, and I pried his hands apart and shook him off, then swung my stick at him to keep him away. I had to get to Kovach, who was in a pile of bodies in front of the net. The referees stayed out of it. They were letting us fight, letting us sort it out by ourselves. They would do this sometimes, just lean against the boards by the penalty box and watch. Larry Lathrop held Dom's top scorer, Marques Ferneaux, long enough for me to get two good shots at his face, without my gloves on. Those in the crowd who hadn't joined us on the ice were on their feet, cheering us on, crazed. When I got to Kovach, he was holding a cheerleader in a tight headlock— she was using both elbows to jab him in the stomach—and I could tell he'd broken his nose again.

Kovach and I got kicked off the team. I had taken a skate in the face—Mack Pellerin, my own teammate, had unintentionally swiped his skate across my eyelid in the pig pile. That night, I had it sewn up—slightly askew, my eyelid swollen and at half-mast—but before I did, Kovach and I looked like real pros for the newspaper cameras, our hair wet, long enough to cover our ears, our faces washed in blood. We looked mean and crazy, and because I was in the foreground, you couldn't tell how short I was. We looked like hockey players.

But that was the end of it. We went to Drama Club. The headmaster told us their numbers were low and they were trying to cast the spring production. We were told if we didn't join up we'd be kicked out of school. Before Kovach and I went to the first rehearsal, we stood in the parking lot behind the main building, and Kovach took out a pack of Winstons. He had cotton in his nostrils and tape across the bridge of his nose. It was snowing.

"Your days as an athlete are over," he said, handing me a cigarette. "We start smoking again today."

I took the cigarette, and he lit it for me.

"Are you ready to become a man?" he asked. Kovach wore his hair like mine, long, parted in the center. Our heroes were Canadian, especially the Buffalo Sabres' flashy first line: Rene Robert, Rick Martin, Gilbert Perreault—the French connection. We used their names as code, as a way to communicate with each other when we wanted to fight, which was often. To throw down the gauntlet, one of us would say "Rene." If the recipient of the challenge thought it was worthy, and was in the mood, he would respond "Rick." Then the aggressor would have another chance, to either reiterate the challenge (to do this, he would respond "Gilbert" and the fighting would commence) or back off, renege on the whole thing by saying nothing. These were our most serious tactics.

"I am a man," I said.

"You're a thug," he said, pushing hair from his eyes. "What I mean is, there's beaver in there." He pointed at the back of the gym, where yellow light glowed from the high windows.

"Yes, I know."

"But the girls in Drama Club, they don't like hockey. They don't care. All that practice, all that pond hockey, it's nothing. With these girls, you're starting from square one."

Kovach did this on occasion: he was saying these things to me, but I knew, really, that he was talking only to himself. I had little experience with girls; I was shy, and he knew that.

"You hear me? These girls are into feelings," he said. "They don't want to know about games you've won, the punches you've landed—that kind of crap. And they don't want to hear you being called FH anymore. It's back to William. And you don't call me Kovach. You call me Danny."

FH is what Coach and all the other players had called me—fire hydrant—as in, Get your damn head in the game, FH, we need a puck in the net. It's how I was built, short and solid.

"Fine."

"You know what I'm saying? Beaver—and I'm talking serious chiquitas in the Drama Club—they don't want a fire hydrant."

"Stuff it, Kovach," I said.

Without uttering *Rene*, he took me out at the knees, but before I fell I grabbed him around the neck so we tumbled together. I elbowed him in the kidneys—a trick I'd mastered on the ice—and he released my legs, but we pretzeled into another stalemate position, both of us breathing hard. At the edge of my vision I could see my watch. "We're late," I said.

When we entered the gym, we brushed the snow off each other, then walked across the sideline of the basketball court to the group, in a circle of orange plastic chairs by the stage. I recognized a few of them; one, Carla Foster, was my dad's star pupil, a very quiet girl with large, purple-framed glasses who ate lunch alone. She was not an actress; she designed sets and ran the lighting. There were two ex-hockey players in the group: Jeremy Bent, a doughy kid, outspoken, with a round face and bad knees. Bent was always on everyone's case, a supreme irritant, always jabbing and snickering and dodging and wheedling. Those of us who knew him made some allowances, tried not to dismiss him entirely, because his father had killed himself, and his mother seemed a bit unhinged; she was a drinker, had been a high-pitched screamer at the hockey games, which was the real reason Bent quit (he blamed it on his knees). The best way to handle Bent was to pretend you were hurt by his teasings, which satisfied him long enough that he'd direct his attentions elsewhere. Also, Bobby Randolf, a kid from Augusta, too thin and delicate for hockey, too mild-mannered. Otherwise I knew no one.

Kovach and I sat down with the group, at the baseline of the court, next to the stage, over the painted words GO VIKINGS and a stern version of Vinnie the Viking, with a sword and battle armor. There were about twenty in the circle. I had known such groups existed at the school. Some on our team called them bottom-feeders, various pockets of unathletic types—the Math Team, Glee Club, and so on—and I had seen Mr. Pritchard in assembly, the enthusiastic faculty adviser of the Drama Club; but typically I had kept my distance. He wore a brown wool three-piece suit and was tall and hollow-cheeked, with gray hair. He pulled out a gold-colored pocket watch, raised an eyebrow, then handed Kovach and me copies of the script.

"The play is *Oliver!*" he said. "Based on the novel *Oliver Twist.*"

Most of the group looked at us with blank expressions, except for Bent, who rolled his eyes.

"The headmaster told me about you two," Mr. Pritchard said. "It just so happens we have space." The way he spoke embarrassed me—he was an aggressive enunciator, and he spoke with a British accent, though I heard he'd grown up in

Springdale, a mill town just ten minutes away. He pointed to Kovach and said, "For today, young sir, please read the part of Bill Sikes." Then he nodded to me, "And you—honest to Christ! What's happened to your eye?"

"Seven stitches, sir," I said. "Got a skate in it."

"Yes. Well. I'd like you to read the part of Noah Claypole," he said, dismayed.

As I opened my script a girl walked in—the girl I came to know as Christina—and she approached the circle, frowning and sighing and flashing her angry, bored eyes in such a way that I felt a tinge of pain in my abdomen. She was like a heron, slender and awkward, and her hair was ordinary, shoulder-length, brown, and messy, and the structures of her face were ordinary, but her eyes were dark and huge. She worried me. I remember not thinking, immediately, that she was beautiful, but that she was alarming-looking, and that I couldn't keep my eyes on her for any sustained period of time without seizing up. She wore a black skirt and black tights and silver bracelets on each wrist. She walked to the stage, crossed her arms on her chest, then turned and stared at all of us, without interest. She wore earrings which swayed on her lobes, and when she rested against the stage, they stopped swaying.

"Hello, Christina," said Mr. Pritchard. "Would you please be so kind as to join us in the circle?"

"I'll stand," she said, and began her vocal warm-ups.

WHAT I LEARNED IN THE WEEKS THAT FOLLOWED WAS THAT Mr. Pritchard loved to demonstrate the dazzling, showstopping numbers—he pretended he didn't, he tried to seem modest, but when he stepped onstage he awkwardly waved his arms and showed us the dance steps, clandestinely thrilled. This inspired me. He knew his body wasn't in step with his mind—you could tell he envisioned perfection, the grace and pizzazz of Fred Astaire, and yet he knew, in his heart, he was a doddering old man—but still, he didn't seem to care that everyone watching was slack-jawed and half asleep, slouching in their chairs. Christina paid attention, of course—she was a real professional—but there was only one Christina, and she was always at odds with Mr. Pritchard, always goading him. He didn't seem threatened by her, though her contention surprised him. I don't think he was used to being challenged: he was so confident and well spoken and British-sounding—not typical fare for the area—that students believed he knew what he was doing. That was always the case in North Allison: if someone was different, it meant they knew something. Christina didn't buy this at all. She'd lived all around the world—in Singapore, in São Paulo, in Copenhagen, in New York City. Her father had recently retired from a long career in banking—he'd opted for the quiet life—Christina was new to our school that year.

She was picked to play Nancy. This casting decision thrilled her. "From what I've gathered, Nancy is borderline schizophrenic," she said, causing Mr. Pritchard to frown. "One minute she's a sweet, nurturing marm—that's when she's with Oliver. The next minute she's a masochistic whore. That's when she's with Sikes." Kovach was cast as Bill Sikes mostly because he was the only boy among us who had a square jaw and brooding eyes, and he was a decent choice for the part; he conveyed an adequate amount of physical threat. The girl originally cast as Oliver caught mono, and I was the only remaining member of the club short enough to take the part. At first I flinched; I didn't want to play such an effeminate role to a public audience in a small, conservative town—but I reminded myself of Kovach's advice, to become a man, and I bucked up. It was, after all, a lead part; I'd be on stage for much of the play, and would have many singing solos. (When he heard my voice, Mr. Pritchard encouraged me to use a method of singing that sounds much like talking.) I secretly enjoyed the song "Where Is Love?," which I told Kovach I hated because of its sentimentality, but really, it made me feel purposeful and legitimate.

Mr. Pritchard never deferred to Christina; her arrogance put him on edge, but he held his ground. For our first rehearsal onstage, Christina had already memorized all of her lines. It was snowing outside, big flakes that fell slowly, and it was early in the afternoon but already dark, and we didn't turn on the gymnasium lights; we worked in the light of the snow-storm, dark blue. Christina bellowed all her lines in a voice that seemed too loud, too deep, staring at the other end of the gym with those huge, serious eyes—she didn't mimic the rhythms of the other readers, and I felt I was in the presence of greatness. Every few pages, Mr. Pritchard would interrupt us to explain how he envisioned the sets, how he planned to block the scenes, and in every case Christina would propose a slight revision, or an entirely alternate route. When she referred to her prior acting experience (at her old school in

New York, she'd once played Lady Macbeth), Mr. Pritchard offered a tight-lipped smile, without responding.

"Wait," said Christina, just when we'd finished Act Three.

"Yes?" asked Mr. Pritchard. His thin lips were chapped and his eyes were small and watery. He was sitting well back from the stage on a wooden stool, and while he waited for Christina to respond, he removed his jacket, then loosened his tie.

"This text is so conflicted," she said. "I felt it in my bones when I was practicing last night."

Bent coughed out a laugh. "Who *is* this?" he asked. "What is her *deal?*" He was reading the part of Mr. Bumble, the tyrannous master of the orphanage.

"My *deal* is acting," she said. "I'm an actress. It's what I do. As in: your *deal* is sitting on the couch and stuffing your face with crap. That's what *you* do."

"Bitch," muttered Bent.

Christina snapped her fingers. "Listen, you troll," she snarled. "Maybe someday you'll know what I'm talking about. You'll know what it means to give a shit. You'll know what it means to be alive."

"Now, now," said Mr. Pritchard. "Let's conserve our energy, shall we? Proceed, Ms. Venturi. Please, I'd like to hear this." He cocked his head slightly to the side and opened his palms to her, smiling, but making it clear—with his eyes— that he loathed her.

"Sikes is an animal, a beautiful wild beast," she said. She flipped hair from her eyes. "Nancy's desire for him is easily understood."

I watched Kovach squirm; he had no reason to feel she was in any way referring to *him*, but I could see how badly he wanted to *be* Sikes, wanted to take on Sikes's wildness, his animal side. Bent was flushed and quiet, but the rest of the cast stared at Christina with empty looks. Bobby Randolf, lying in the wings, was asleep, as was Ed Latvis, our baby-faced Fagin.

"Oliver, on the other hand," said Christina. "What's the story? We all know he's cute, and somewhat pathetic, but why is she so fascinated? Why does she care?"

At this, I felt my legs go dead. "Well, Christina, he's an orphan," said Mr. Pritchard. "And Nancy feels like a mother to him."

"Come on," she said. "That's a bit simplistic, wouldn't you say? I think we need to play up the sex."

"Sex? He's a young boy," said Mr. Pritchard, pointing at me.

"He's an adolescent," said Christina.

"I'm a senior," I said.

"You're a putz," said Bent.

"He's very young, and innocent, and he doesn't have a mother," said Mr. Pritchard.

"But he's also verging on manhood," said Christina. "When he sings that song, 'Where Is Love?'—well, what do you think that means, Mr. Pritchard?"

"What do I *think* it means?" he asked. "Gracious, I know exactly what it means."

"Adolescent boys are disoriented by their libido. He doesn't know where love is," said Christina. "I think Nancy should show him."

"Let's remember what this play is about," said Mr. Pritchard.

"What is it about?" asked Christina.

"It's about . . . well, this is a story based on a novel by Charles Dickens, for heaven's sake . . . I think it's safe to assume he didn't intend for Nancy to have sexual feelings for Oliver."

"Now, Mr. Pritchard," she said. "I think Oliver has ideas about love, he knows what it is, he just doesn't know why any of it isn't coming his way." She walked across the stage to me and touched her hand lightly to my cheek. Then she said, "We need to make people feel. That's what the stage is all about. We need to grab them."

"You remember, of course, that I am the director," said Mr. Pritchard, standing, smiling again. "I'll be the one deciding what we need to do."

This, we all suspected, was a false statement.

I was frozen. I had my hands jammed in my brown corduroy pants and my face was ablaze. What did this mean? What was she saying? I would be Oliver, I was Oliver, I was verging on manhood, I would find love, I knew where it was, I was an actor, she was an actress, I was ready, I would rise to the occasion, I would sing every word and speak every line for her, every gesture would be hers, for her and by her and of her—I couldn't look at her. I stared at Mr. Pritchard. He looked tired and thin.

"Ha!" cried Bent, pointing at me. "Christ!"

"That's quite enough, Jeremy," said Mr. Pritchard, raising his voice. Then he walked slowly toward the stage. He massaged his chin in mock concentration. "Okay, Ms. Venturi, I'm trying to understand. But I have to admit, I'm not sure what this has to do with the play. Are you proposing we change the script?"

"No," she said. "I mean . . . yes, of course I am. This script is nearly unreadable. But I understand the circumstances. I understand I'm in a Drama Club, and there are rules."

"Indeed," said Mr. Pritchard.

"But the play can be more complex than what we find on the page. We can bring our own emotions to it," she said.

"It's called Method acting," said Kovach, and Christina turned to him and smiled. It was a trick Kovach had, and I envied him for it: he always knew the right thing to say. He was usually quiet in public, but when he spoke, he made it count. People listened to him because of his eyes, and his muscles. Everyone but Bent.

"What do *you* know, Kovach," said Bent.

"Cram it, Bent," he said.

"Whoa there," said Mr. Pritchard. The way I felt about Kovach was that he was better than I was—more composed and confident—which is not to say he didn't still have a long way to go.

"Method acting. That's exactly what it's called," said Christina. "We used it at my old school. Dr. McCollough—he was my director for *Macbeth*—he used to say, *no emotion should pass unused.* I got some great mileage out of thoughts I'd been carrying around, you know, about anger and violence and revenge."

We heard the muffled sounds of a snowplow scraping its way across the parking lot. Ed Latvis seemed to wake—he rolled over—and then it was quiet again.

"Thank you, Christina. I'm sure your advice will come in handy. Kids, you hear what she's saying?" asked Mr. Pritchard.

I nodded, as did Kovach, and the others mumbled in agreement. When Mr. Pritchard did that—called us "kids"—Christina turned sharply away, pushed her hair behind her ears, which gave me a chance to look at her closely, without fear of being caught. When I stared at her then, in profile—at her delicate chin and long neck, at her fierce eyes—I suspected there were things she knew which I would never know, differences between us I would never be able to accept or understand. I was wrecked.

THAT NIGHT, I STAYED IN THE SHOWER FOR A LONG TIME, letting the water beat against my head and scald my skin. I plugged the drain and let the water rise over my feet and my ankles, keeping my eyes closed, trying to summon Christina's face. But I couldn't. All I got was a burning in my stomach, and a sinking feeling that when I opened my eyes and stepped from the bathroom, I'd realize that Christina had never come to Drama Club, that I'd dreamed her, and that tomorrow I'd be faced with Bent and all the rest, nothing more. Or that I'd be back on the team, still fighting and getting slammed against the boards. Perhaps my greatest fear, though, was that she was someone I'd actually contend with, and that she'd find out I was a worm with nothing to offer, forcing me to slither back underground, alone. She was an actress—an artist—and I was a short ex-hockey player whose father taught geometry. I sat down in the tub and let the shower thunder down around me, until the water reached the overflow drain and I opened my eyes.

I got dressed and went to the basement, where, when I was ten, I'd made a sturdy goal out of PVC piping. I took slap shots from twenty yards away, the full length of the basement, dribbling the puck on the shiny cement. I called corners of the net— top left, bottom right—and placed my shots, dead on.

Practicing my shot made me want to go back and visit the locker room, where I'd spent hours which added up to days, months—a lifetime. It was ours; Coach rarely entered, he saved his speeches for the bench. When we were sophomores, a naked Bent—he hadn't yet made the switch to drama— asked me in front of the entire squad if I would rather suck my dad's dick or have my dad suck mine, and instead of quickly dismissing the question, I lingered, stumped. It was at the end of a labyrinth of tunnels in the rink, and when I was down there, I couldn't shake the thought that I belonged, that I was comforted by the darkness, the isolation. We called it the Thunderdome when we wrestled, wearing shin guards and helmets, sturdy garter belts to hold up our hockey socks—*two men enter, one man leaves.* It was where I'd been dazzled by the sight of Bobby Randolf's blood—in a game against Lewiston, he'd gotten a stick up under the cage of his helmet in the second period, ripping open his chin. His blood covered the front of his orange jersey. Bobby was quiet and shy, thin-limbed and bookish—not much of a hockey player and altogether uncomfortable with the way he moved in the world. He looked apologetic for his bleeding, but it got me jazzed up for the final period; I scored two more goals and we won the game.

After an hour of slap shots, Kovach and I met up by the Royal River for a smoke. We lived in neighboring apartments on campus, in the woods by the river—we'd been living in faculty housing our whole lives. Before we learned about the chemicals being dumped by the paper mill in Springdale, we spent much of our time in the summer swimming in the Royal, but in the winter it bubbled under ice not thick enough to skate on.

"You like her, don't you?" I asked. The snow had stopped; the sun had set hours earlier, but the sky was a dark orange, the light from Springdale. We threw snowballs at the trunk of a big oak tree down the hill from the apartment complex.

"She seems fine," said Kovach. "But I think you should go after her." He had a better handle on talking and smoking and throwing snowballs all at once than I did. He wore a blue hunting cap which kept his hair out of his eyes, and a jean jacket, the same kind as mine, but lighter in color—the preferred style. I had a better arm, could blow more smoke with my throws, but Kovach was accurate. Kovach lobbed them with arc and they usually smacked the trunk, leaving a pill of white on the bark.

"She's probably more your type," I said.

"You see the way she called off Bent?" he asked.

"Incredible," I said.

"You *troll*. I like that."

"Amazing."

"Not really amazing," said Kovach. "Just very, very cool."

"Amazing in the coolest sense," I said.

"Right."

"One of us should go after her," I said. The snow was too dry to pack well—many of the snowballs I cupped in my gloves disappeared when I threw them.

"One or the other."

"But one of us, definitely."

"What the hell, right?" he said.

"Right."

"But the thing is—with *this* girl, it might not matter," said Kovach. "I mean, come on. Neither of us is going to get her, so I say let's not worry too much about it."

"You like her," I said.

"Go ahead and like her," said Kovach. "That's fine."

"Jesus, it's true. You really want to put the puck in the net." I slung a chunk of ice sidearm that whistled past the elm and landed well down the bank.

"If you weren't so freakishly small, FH, I'd pound you. Be my guest, go after her."

"And you'd be fine with it?"

"I told you, cock sore, I'm fine."

"Fine," I said.

"Great."

"Great?" I asked.

"I'll pound you, FH, if you say one more word." He was looking solemnly down the bank at the frozen river.

I mimed a slow-motion slap shot. "Puck . . . in . . . net," I said.

"*Rene,*" said Kovach.

"*Rick,*" I said. My neck tensed, and I could already see my first move—I'd grab his right leg and sweep the left one.

"*Gilbert,*" said Kovach, and our gloves were off.

As hockey players, we spent many hours in the weight room, and the time hadn't been wasted on either of us. Kovach used his taller frame to great advantage, keeping me at bay with his long arms, but when we hit the snow, my shorter, stronger arms could crank his torso—he never got me on my back.

After—I'd refouled Kovach's nose, the stitches in my eyelid were burning, and he'd gotten me in the mouth with an elbow—we lay in the snow, exhausted.

"So, it's decided," said Kovach.

"That's right, it's decided," I said.

A gust of wind blew through the woods, and snow from the branches above sprayed down on our hot faces.

"What?" said Kovach.

"What do you mean, *what?*"

"Make yourself clear," he said.

"Haven't I?"

"So neither of us," he said, holding his nose in his hands, "neither of us will go for her."

"Okay," I said. "You really mean that?"

"You were the one who said it."

"I said it first. But now you've said it, too."

"Right," said Kovach.

"Right."

"Okay?"

"Okay."

"So there it is, Boitano," he said. "It's decided." To call someone by the name of a figure skater—that was heavy artillery.

"Oh, you bet," I said, and we didn't say another word. We walked up the hill, clear of each other, and every ten yards or so I spat blood from my lip in the snow.

I didn't like being at odds with Kovach, and I held only a vague hope of finding love with Christina, but there was something thrilling about walking up the hill spitting blood in the snow, holding my ground in this standoff with Kovach. It's a rare shot in the arm—to feel, in a moment, your life unfolding like that, to understand how your actions can change you for good.

CHRISTINA WAS NOT SOMEONE I SAW IN THE HALLS, OR WAITING for the bus, and we had no classes together; I hadn't seen her outside of rehearsal since she'd started at the academy. It was hard to imagine her doing other things—taking a physics class, for example, or sitting through study hall. The idea of her having parents, people to whom she related outside the realm of *Oliver!*, was difficult to muster, too. While I knew she did in fact have a family, that she actually did things off the stage, could speak words in a normal voice, her *Oliver!* persona was plenty for me. At the beginning, I was too timid to seek her out otherwise.

We were already in the third week of rehearsals, but we were still walking through the blocking of each scene, so that Mr. Pritchard could make adjustments—this seemed overly mechanical, and I myself was beginning to question his judgment, wondering if he wasn't just faking it all, this care and precision. What could it possibly matter if the girl selling roses stopped *six* times or if she stopped *seven* times in her march across the stage? Christina had convinced me: it was better for the action of the play to bubble up from unknown places. Still, I hadn't yet spoken directly to her—I had spoken to her as Oliver, only. I caught her eye on a few occasions, but when this happened, she neither looked away quickly nor held my gaze, which didn't give me much hope. Her attentions were focused on Kovach; he was someone else I wasn't talking to.

For the blocking of the scenes, Mr. Pritchard asked the principals to stand in the wings, just behind the curtains, and minor characters could sit in the audience. Kovach, as Bill Sikes, was certainly a minor character, not appearing much until the end of the play. But he stood by the curtain ropes with his hands clasped, resting on his belt, listening patiently to Christina as she talked on and on to him, in a whisper, sometimes touching his arm for emphasis. I watched from the opposite wing, with Bent.

"Check that out," Bent said. "He's lunch."

"You think?" I asked, though it was obvious. I could tell Kovach was trying to be charming, but he looked like a zombie.

"Hell, yes," said Bent.

"Is she buying it?" I asked.

"She's got to think he's a bullshit artist," said Bent. "Watch his hands. He looks like a fucking nun." Kovach shook away the hair that fell in front of his eyes.

"He can hardly keep it together, poor guy," I said. "I say he cracks pretty soon, starts throwing pucks at her head."

Kovach was nodding and smiling—then he unclasped his hands and folded his arms across his chest, furrowing his brow.

"Bullshit artist," said Bent.

"Makes you wonder about Christina, doesn't it?"

"Sure does."

"Makes you wonder if she's knows what she's dealing with."

"Absolutely."

It was tough to discern, though, exactly what was going on. I had no reason to think this way, but I couldn't imagine Christina liking anyone but me—and I had only spoken to her on a few occasions, always for practical reasons: *Could you hand me that script? Is the break over? We've changed that scene—now you come in from the left.* It was dawning on me, though, that it was possible I was a bottom-feeder in her eyes—a faculty kid, unsophisticated, a townie. When Mr. Pritchard asked Christina and me to take the stage, to walk through the musical number "I'd Do Anything," he stood up from his stool to dodder through the steps. She scoffed—and then he described some of the other flourishes he'd come up with—twirling umbrellas and juggling top hats and flashing petticoats, and she said, loudly, "This is awful."

But Mr. Pritchard had begun to ignore her entirely. "Okay, join hands, you two," he said. "And we'll walk through it."

The way to play that moment, in front of Kovach and Bent and Bobby and the rest, was to make it seem as though holding Christina's hand was as ordinary as anything else I did in the course of a usual day, as casual and unconscious as shooting slap shots or eating cereal. And as a senior in high school, nearly old enough to vote and be drafted, I wanted to believe this, too. But Christina offered solid proof that life was a series of terrifying events, of grave and immediate result. I wanted to puke or, better yet, walk to the wings and punch Kovach, but I reached out and took her hand instead.

What happened surprised me.

I heard the buzz of the lights in the rafters, and I felt no fear, I felt nothing at all.

I turned and looked at her and said, "Hey."

"Hey," she said.

"Hey, what's up?" I said.

"Can you ease up with your grip there, sweetie?" she said.

Mr. Pritchard asked us to walk backwards to stage right, holding hands, and then skip in unison across the stage, stop, turn, then skip our way back across. All of this went smoothly. We did it seven or eight times, and by the end Mr. Pritchard was smiling a big embarrassing grin, standing next to his stool, applauding. Christina glanced at me, then at our hands—she was ready for me to let go—but before I did, I said, "You like hockey?"

"No," she said.

"You like hot dogs?"

"No," she said.

She was taller than me, probably three or four inches, and she was smirking, so I shivered.

"You should come to the game tonight. I think you'd like it."

"Well, the industry of sports appalls me, so I doubt you're

right." Up close, I saw a small pimple on her nose, which gave me hope. But she had her hair gathered in an elastic, sprouting from the top of her head, and she wore enough dark eye makeup that I felt insecure about the polyester sweat suit I was wearing, with stripes on the arms and the legs.

"You're new here, right?" I said. "Hockey is very *Maine*. You should get to know the place." I held on to her hand.

She looked over at the wings, in Kovach's direction—but Kovach had left. She said, "What time?"

"You sure?" I asked.

"Let me tell you a secret, FH," she said. "When a girl says yes, don't ask her if she's sure."

I knew this was Kovach's way of challenging me, but I didn't want to overreact. I sat down on the edge of the stage, and she sat down with me.

"Did he tell you to call me that?" I asked, in my calmest voice. I wanted to say more, but all I could think about was making Kovach bleed, rebreaking his crooked nose. That would have been the surest way, really, to calm me down.

"He said that's what your mother calls you," she said. "I like it. It adds to your *persona* as an actor."

"My mother doesn't call me FH," I said. I looked at my hands, the small white scars on the knuckles. Kovach was a dead man.

THAT NIGHT, I WENT LOOKING FOR HIM. I TRIED ALL THE usual places—the flooded spot by the underpass where we skated, the desolate snow fields behind the school where kids gathered to sniff ScotchGard. I ended up at the 7-Eleven talking to Bent, who was holding court by the ice cooler outside the store. On the well-lit blacktop in front, middle school kids rode their banana-seated bicycles. The Sev-Lev parking lot was like an airstrip; for hours on a Friday night you could watch them taxi in, glance around, then speed off again into the night. That's the way it was all year round, even with the snow. Bent waited by the ice machine and from time to time would ask one of the bicycle riders—one he'd seen playing peewee hockey, or one with an older sibling in our class—to approach him, set their kickstands down, and take a punch in the arm, or a dead leg.

"You seen Kovach?" I asked Bent. I stood next to him, with my back against the store.

"He's probably back home, poking his mom," he said.

"You seen Christina?" I asked.

"She's up at your house, getting it from your dad."

I looked at Bent as he scanned the parking lot, following the middle schoolers with his eyes.

"Bent, why are you out here? You still get off beating up these pygmies?" I asked, but as hard as I tried to separate myself from Bent's sadistic ways, I knew we were cut from the same cloth.

"St. Clair!" he yelled. A small kid I didn't recognize—he wore a hat with a pom-pom and wool mittens, and he was riding a bicycle much too big for him—pedaled over to us.

"Park," said Bent.

St. Clair dismounted and stood cowering in front of us. Bent cocked back his arm and threw a jab—stopping just short of St. Clair's head, but the kid buckled anyway.

"Don't *ever* flinch like that," said Bent. "Now beat cheeks."
He pushed the kid, who tripped over his feet and fell into his
bicycle, knocking it over. Bent laughed.

When St. Clair picked himself up again, I came at him
with a fist, but this time he held his ground. I raised my chin
to him, in approval. "If you see Kovach," I said, "tell him I
need to talk to him." St. Clair shrugged. Bent was still staring
and scowling at him, waiting for him to ride away. When St.
Clair got his feet back on the pedals, he pumped his way off
the blacktop and into the night.

"Pussy, pussy, pussy," yelled Bent. "You keep on riding."

I needed to find Kovach, bad. The whole thing was making me panic. But when St. Clair came back into the lot at full
speed, buzzing us, giving us the finger as he passed, then
completing a victory lap with a smile on his face, Bent was
apoplectic, and I realized that to get to Kovach, there were
other, less conventional tactics I could use. Fighting had
always been my first card; I had seen how well it worked on
the ice, to get your opponents thinking less about the puck
and more about your knuckles cracking their teeth, but
Kovach wasn't cowed by fighting. Hurting him was one
thing—I still had that capacity—but after seeing him with
Christina, I knew where to aim next.

IT WAS A HOME GAME AT THE ACADEMY, AGAINST BIDDEFORD,
a weak team with a reputation for rough play. I borrowed my
father's Eskimo jacket, which had a fur-lined hood and made
me look especially sharp, and taller—it came down to my
knees. While I waited in the parking lot for Christina, I felt

like a veteran, having matured past my hockey phase, my days of towel-snapping in the locker room, and I realized that Christina was right: I was building a persona; I was an actor, the lead in a play. It was dark and cold—the snowiest winter in memory, we'd already gotten over five feet—and I stood in the light cast by one of the towering fluorescents near the entrance of the rink as the crowd filed in, the mothers with the milk jugs, younger brothers and sisters wearing knitted orange caps, fathers with their hands in the pockets of their varsity jackets. All around me, plows had pushed the snow into piles twice my size.

Christina showed up only a few minutes late wearing a sheepskin cap which matched the lining of my father's jacket—a good sign—and her brown hair peeked out the sides of the hat, shiny and uneven, not tucked behind her ears. This seemed both conspicuous and accidental—either way, it struck me as the most beautiful thing I'd ever seen. I was nervous and felt inclined to talk about the cold weather, or the large number of people attending the game, but these were silly, obvious things to say, so I kept quiet. We got inside just before the puck dropped, squeezing our way into the bleachers behind the visitors' net, and I felt the eyes of the crowd. Is it presumptuous to say that people were watching me closely as I climbed the bleachers? Perhaps. But my attendance at that game was in some small way a statement to those who'd loved my fighting ways: I wasn't ashamed of what I'd done at St. Dominic's. And by escorting the lovely Christina, I was also rebutting all those in the crowd who saw me as a heartless, bloodthirsty goon: I was capable of love.

The games against Biddeford were packed because we always beat them, and there were always fights. Biddeford's coach was a legend, a guy named Harold Prud'homme—Hospital Harry—who'd made his name in the AHL by cross-checking opponents in the neck.

Christina kept her arms folded in front of her and she shifted her weight from foot to foot—but the rest of the crowd seemed restless, too: the game started slowly; the players were patiently passing the puck around—clack, clack, clack—and there was little contact, no penalties, and no goals scored. But everyone—except Christina—knew what was coming. I was watching Biddeford's star center, number 11, a fair-skinned kid with a wispy blond mustache. He, like most players in the league, was quick-reflexed, sinewy, and as ruthless and stubborn as a table saw. At every face-off, as he bent over waiting for the referee to drop the puck, he'd pretend to lose his balance. He'd heave his weight forward and bang his helmet against the guy across from him. Every time. The referee was choosing not to blow his whistle, for now.

"The ref beats his wife," someone yelled.

I knew the head-banging wouldn't be tolerated for long, so I leaned over to Christina and whispered, "Keep an eye on number eleven."

"What do you think I am?" she asked. "I've seen hockey before."

"Watch," I said. "This guy's old school. A real puckhead. He's like his coach." I wanted to show her something she wasn't expecting.

At the next face-off—he was in our zone, we had a perfect

view of him—he did the helmet-banging trick, then collected himself and looked up. His mustache wiggled—a nervous habit I remembered fondly from my playing days.

"Watch," I said.

The referee held the puck over the two players' sticks. They glided away from each other slightly, and the ref hesitated.

"Ready."

The kid flared his nostrils and the mustache twitched again.

"Set."

The players straightened their backs, dropped their sticks, and the crowd rose to its feet.

"Here it is," I whispered.

We heard the quiet, delicate sound of their gloves hitting the ice before the crowd took a big breath in. Then, of course, everyone was screaming. The benches emptied; the two players had removed their helmets, and before the ref could get between them, Mack Pellerin had number 11's jersey over his head and was flurrying punches at his ribs.

I folded my arms on my chest and cheered them on, and when their coach stepped onto the ice and shuffled in dress shoes toward the melee, I chanted with the rest of the crowd, "HOS-PIT-AL!" (clap), "HOS-PIT-AL!" (stomp), "HOS-PIT-AL!" (clap).

Christina was standing, too, but she was quiet, staring with her serious eyes at the fray.

"Oh," I said. "I'm sorry. You must not like this."

She said nothing.

"It's okay," I said. "They'll all be okay. You don't really get that hurt—it's mostly just teeth and noses."

She held the back of my coat, clenching the fabric in her fist. "Now, this guy—he used to be a player?" she asked

"That's Hospital Harry. He used to play for Maine."

Harry was yelling at the ref, who stood in front of him with his hands on his hips until Harry touched him—a finger to the chest. Then the ref swatted Harry's arm away and Harry landed a swift roundhouse to the ref's jaw. Christina pulled at the back of my coat. "Nice hit," she said.

The other fans in the bleachers were screaming and banging their feet. Most of the players were paired off, with their fists raised, circling each other like magnets. Some were down on the ice, pulling at each other's jerseys. I caught the eyes of my old linemate Larry Lathrop, who smiled up at me, a big, full-faced grin: his teeth were bright red.

"You used to do this?" She pointed at the ice.

"Yup," I said.

"And you really punched people?" she asked.

"I punched a lot of people," I said.

"So you were a puckhead?" she said.

"I was," I said.

"There's actually something to it," she said. "It's totally unscripted. But full of feeling and struggle." When she said this, I experienced a swell of recognition—she was spot on, and I saw the fight, this performance, with new eyes. We watched Larry Lathrop take a victory lap around the ice, whipping a Biddeford jersey in a circle over his head like a lasso. Lathrop, God bless him: he was a fantastic puckhead—perhaps the best now, with Kovach gone—and this didn't bother me, I no longer wanted what he had. With Christina talking to me in this way, I felt as though I'd actually changed—I had a new set of concerns. I was, after all, an actor now.

THAT NIGHT, IN THE JANITOR'S CLOSET OF MY APARTMENT complex, beside mop buckets and toolboxes, I kissed her, and when she kissed me back, she bit my tongue, then sucked on it, clamping down around it with her lips and yanking it with the strength of her lungs. I took her coat off, and she unzipped my pants, so I removed her sweater and unbuttoned the outermost of three shirts she was wearing. I tried to respond to each move she made with an action I hoped she'd find interesting, original, unclichéd. When she kissed me on the eyelid, where my scar was, I put my pinkie in her navel, but she squirmed, telling me it made her feel sick.

I pulled the two other shirts she was wearing over her head, but she told me she was cold, so I put one of them back on, and I put another one of them only half on, just around her neck, like a scarf. Then I took her pants off, and I got her thermals to her knees, but again she said she was cold, so I pulled them back up with great care, making sure I didn't pull them too far up, and with my hands in the waistband, I felt for her underwear, in the back. My fingers brushed the tag, which was silky, making me feel grateful—I was so glad her clothes were comfortable. In celebration, I carefully rested a finger on the soft spot at the top of the crack of her ass.

We lay pressed against each other in the dark, kissing, biting. It was one-thirty in the morning, but I was wired. Where had I gotten the courage to take her in my arms like this? I decided, at that moment, that we would never leave the closet.

With the janitor's tools, I would fashion a slot in the door so my father could deliver us food. "You okay?" she asked.

"I love you," I said.

"No," she said. "You're totally out of it right now, I can tell. You're just euphoric, that's all. This is what happens with me, to boys. Just wait it out—it'll pass."

"I don't think so," I said.

"Yes," she said. She seemed angry. "Stop thinking about me, about me as Christina. Think about Nancy—and I'll think about Oliver. It's much better that way."

I sat up, propping my arm on a mop bucket. "But I feel like I really, really know you." And that was the truth.

She put her cold hand down my pants and I trapped it between my thighs. "You're confused," she said. "This isn't anything like fighting—it's not about how you feel. At this point it's more like eating, or shoveling the driveway—something like that."

She opened the closet door. In the light of the hallway, being with Christina felt temporary, and this depressed me. She asked me to walk her home, across town. Outside, the temperature had dropped even further, a sharp cold which amplified sound. Even under layers and layers of clothes, I felt naked to the world. The wind made my eyes water, which sharpened my vision, and our boots crunched the sandy ice on the sidewalks. She'd pulled her fur hat down over her eyebrows.

"Is there something going on between you and Kovach?" I asked.

"Who am I with?" she asked.

"You're with me," I said.

"And who is Kovach not with?" she asked.

This took me a second to figure out. Then I said, "He's . . . not with you."

She squeezed my hand.

She was right. I was with her then, and right then only; that's how it was with her. The thought of the two of us in the closet, the perfection of that arrangement, I could still feel it, even with the stinging air blowing in our faces. The thing was, being with her—being in close proximity to her—meant that I was ruined. Just a few weeks earlier, any thoughts of Christina made me feel as though I was living my life in quick, exhilarating bursts. But after walking her home that night, I forced myself not to think about her, because to think about her was to understand there'd be a day when it all would be over. Maybe it would be the day I died—even so, this was devastating to consider. To be euphoric was to pay a price—it always got me thinking of the end. I was seventeen and strong, but she was leveling me, burning me from the top floor down.

WE HAD ONE EVERY YEAR—THEY CALLED IT JANUARY THAW— but when it came just days before the performance, it scared me shitless. It seemed mean-spirited, that warm air, getting some of us in T-shirts, letting us open our windows, wash the grime from our cars, take walks for the joy of it. I was wary of this delusion—that during the darkest days of the year, we all felt limber and happy. Without ice on the state roads, drivers picked up their speed, surprising deer and moose who'd flooded the shoulders, hungry for salt—every year, around this time, there was carnage, and the wind smelled like blood.

The first day of thaw I ran through my lines in the basement. There'd been a rumor circulating that the hockey players were ruining the play; none of us could act, people said; we were just brutes, taking up space onstage. I knew I could prove this rumor wrong if I practiced enough. In the basement I got into character by putting on my pauper's cap and bringing Christina to mind. This hurt; it made me feel like I was getting my innards spooled out of me, inch by inch, but it was the only way I could make the lines sing. I closed the sliding windows near the ceiling to keep the warm wind out; my eyes were open, and I was entranced.

The fact was, Christina was unlike anyone I'd ever met. There'd been girls I'd liked in the past, but in comparison to Christina—her stubbornness, her huge, knowing eyes, the fact that she'd lived in other parts of the world, the way she bit me when we kissed—all the other girls seemed silly and utterly replaceable. Even as I practiced my lines from the first scene, before Oliver had any knowledge of Nancy's existence, I wanted to envision Christina—and that lovely soft spot at the top of the crack of her ass. There I was, an orphan, getting gruel spooned into my bowl. But it wasn't enough. It had never been enough. As Christina had said, I needed to trust the moment, respond to my feelings, speak the lines accordingly. In my mind I saw Mr. Bumble, smiling wickedly. And there was Christina, with the second of three shirts draped around her neck, saying she was cold. "Please, sir . . . I want some *more*," I said.

Just then, something flashed in the corner of my vision, something moving outside. I looked up to see Kovach in the window near the ceiling staring down at me, but as soon as I caught sight of him, he was gone.

IT WAS BENT WHO BROUGHT THE NEWS, THOUGH I KNEW IT was coming. I was in the Sev-Lev, looking to shoplift. I wasn't eating much those days—couldn't eat like I used to, when I was a hockey player—and with only three days before the performance, candy bars were the only food that appealed to me. Also, I had to steal them. That's what Christina had done to me; I felt inverted, insane. A willingness to be punished was the only feeling that made any sense to me.

"Psst," he said. "FH."

I was lingering in the center aisle, peering at the round mirror in the corner of the store, keeping an eye on the clerk behind the counter.

"Piss off," I said. "I'm busy."

But he told me anyway.

"Christina and Kovach, they're doing it," said Bent.

"How would you know?"

"She told me."

"You're a bullshit artist."

"She told me because she knew I'd tell you."

"That's ridiculous," I said, but I knew it wasn't. The cashier turned to fetch a package of cigarillos, so I made my move—three Baby Ruths into the front pocket of my sweat-shirt. I walked with Bent to the counter and bought two one-cent pieces of Bazooka—then walked out of the store.

Bent was wearing shorts and flip-flops—it was in the forties and sunny; the parking lot was a delta of snowmelt. Water was converging from places all over town, flowing to the sewers on Main Street. For a brief second, I looked at Bent—his big smile, his fat face, his Bermuda shorts, surrounded by all that melting snow—and I thought he was the devil. I grabbed him by the front of his T-shirt and pulled him close, standing tiptoe to look him in the eyes.

"Christ," he said. "It's not my fault."

Through clenched teeth, I said, "I know," but I continued to hold him there, staring.

"Just because I told you doesn't mean I'm the one who's fucking your girlfriend," he said.

"I know," I said, releasing him. Worst of all was that it wasn't a surprise, this news—not at all. I had known from the beginning it would end. Actually, it had never really started. For Bent to call her my "girlfriend" felt like an elbow to the chops.

I knew that at our dress rehearsal, Kovach wouldn't be able to avoid me—we were on stage at the same time for one brief scene, near the end of the play, when Sikes stabs Nancy and then Sikes gets shot, and we all trundle offstage together, before curtain call. In anticipation of this scene, Christina rubbed my shoulders in the wings off stage left, whispering "I'd do anything" slowly and softly in my ear, her nose warm in my hair. I knew she was lying, but it didn't matter. She was next to me and it felt amazing, it felt like I was being filled with some kind of hot, soothing liquid. Outside, it rained, and through the window of the gym Christina and I watched a large sheet of snow slip off the roof and thunder to the ground.

After the scene, Kovach jumped up from playing dead, and I met him in the wings. "I know all about it," I said.

"You don't know anything," he said.

I taunted him with a vicious *Rene.* He said, "That's over."

"You're just euphoric," I said. "That's what happens with her. It'll pass."

"Use that anger," he said. As part of his costume, Kovach hadn't shaved for a week. His whiskers were as dark as his eyes.

"What's gotten into you," I said, shoving him. "*Rene.*"

"I've got a play to do," he said. "That's what's gotten into me. I'm trying to be Sikes—that's all I'm concerned with now."

"Jesus. You're buying that crap? I know just what she's been saying," I said. "*Think about Nancy. It's better that way.*"

He tilted his head back and shook the hair from his eyes. "Did she talk to you?"

"Use that anger," I said, and I tipped my little pauper's cap to him and walked out to take a bow.

THE GYMNASIUM LIGHTS WERE DIMMED ON THE NIGHT OF the play; Mr. Pritchard pinned a white carnation to the lapel of his dark blue suit; the ushers, seventh- and eighth-grade Drama Club aspirants, stood by the door in dark suits and long black dresses with white carnations, too, handing out programs, helping the elderly to their seats. They were just little kids, really, and their clothes were ill fitting, but I envied them, the innocent excitement they must have felt. I wasn't excited; I was calmed by the grim knowledge of my lot. I hadn't slept at all the night before—down in my basement, I'd stared at the ceiling, smoking cigarettes while saying my lines, over and over.

Cold weather had returned without apology. Arctic air blew down from Quebec; the ground, tricked into thawing during the previous week, was like granite again, as were the ponds. For most of the town, this was great news—it was a hockey town, after all, and most backyards had a flooded spot, with boards and nets. These little rinks were perfect now. But tonight, everyone had postponed their skating plans—they had come for the play. Even the hockey team was there— Larry Lathrop, Mack Pellerin, all of them. I was in the wings, peeking through the curtains, watching the rows of plastic chairs fill with people—when Christina came up from behind me and rested her chin on my shoulder.

"It's our night, sweetie. They're all here for us." She kissed me softly on the neck.

I couldn't look at her—but I couldn't shrug her off, either. Just before I took my place, Mr. Pritchard left his seat in the front row to come backstage for a word with me.

"They'll like it," he said. "I know they'll like it. I just want to suggest, William, that you keep it under control."

"Yes sir," I said.

"What I mean is, I know how tough she can be," he said.

"Yes, sir," I said.

"But I must say, William, I trust your instincts," he said. "Your instincts, they're sound. Make sure that they're *yours*, though. Don't let her bully you," he said.

"Okay, sir," I said.

"You've got the opportunity to bring something special to these people, William," he said.

"Yes," I said.

"Break a leg," he said, and he tapped his knuckles against my arm. Then he was gone.

I liked Pritchard; he had a good heart.

When the curtain rose, the lights were hot on my face and I couldn't see the audience—it was perfect this way; I was fully entranced. In fact, during the first scene—the gruel scene—the cocoon of stage lights allowed me to take an opportunity I might otherwise have avoided. When Mr. Bumble ordered Oliver to be seized, I didn't run away from the other orphans. I did what came naturally: I squared off with them, raising my fists. This caused surprise and confusion among my fellow actors, who shied away, except for Bobby Randolf, who, when he saw me charging, assumed I'd veer away at the last second. I didn't. I came at him like a night train, and in one swift motion slapped my hands on his shoulders and landed a quick knee to his groin. He crumpled like a bird shot from the sky. The audience was surprised, I could tell. Then I heard someone—perhaps Mack Pellerin—say "*Nice!*"

Bent was next. He figured I couldn't take it further, but he guessed wrong. Oliver was this beast inside of me, an orphan *terrible*, so unlike the character I'd met just six weeks earlier. I wasn't sure how it was playing to the audience, but as Christina said, I had to trust my emotions. That was part of the deal. So I caught Bent with an uppercut, just below the rib cage. Eventually, the rest of the orphans figured out that I was merely ad-libbing, and seven of them hauled me offstage. The scene ended. The crowd applauded riotously.

Christina met me offstage. "You're feeling it, aren't you," she said.

"Yes. Yes, I am." I took her hand, brought her fingers to my lips, but before I could kiss them, she pulled them away.

"Sweetie, it's showtime," she said, and pushed me gently toward the stage. I was back on.

Much of the play went as planned—though Bent, who played both Mr. Bumble and one of Fagin's pickpockets, decided to get me back for the body blow I'd landed in Act One by sucker-punching me in Act Three—I picked myself up, brushed myself off, and didn't retaliate. I was proud of Bent for this flourish—he was feeling it, too.

It wasn't until the end, though, when Sikes went on his rampage, that the muse really struck, showering us with inspiration like fairy dust. Sikes—Kovach, that is—was supposed to take a knife to Nancy, and then kidnap me while on the run from the angry mob. But as Kovach raised his knife above Nancy's head, I ran from the wings off stage left and tackled him. The audience loved this—I knew they would—not many in North Allison had read the novel, and I knew they craved a happy ending. Kovach was so surprised by this that I easily swiped the knife from his sweaty hands. But what I did next surprised him even more. I thrust the knife into his neck.

"Down with Sikes!" I screamed, and the audience screamed, too—they were right there with me, really wanting Sikes to get it. Mr. Pritchard had put enough stickum on the heel of the retractable blade that it stuck beautifully to Kovach's glistening neck, like the finger of God.

Kovach was too dignified an actor to try to ad-lib his way out of that one. With the knife handle on his neck, though, he was given a moment to shine: he staggered and coughed and wheezed and collapsed with a thud to the stage. When the angry mob charged in from the wings off stage right, they had less reason to be angry—Sikes was dead, after all, and Nancy was standing next to me, very much alive. They weren't as quick as Kovach had been to roll with my plot change, so I took charge, once again. I yelled, "Down with Sikes!" pointing at the supine Kovach, and they yelled it back at me, "Down with Sikes!"—in fact, everyone in the audience yelled it, too.

Then I took Christina into my arms. Wow, she really looked amazing, then. Ask anyone from North Allison; they remember. That tattered emerald dress with cream-colored petticoat, her flushed cheeks and naked arms and those enormous, life-changing eyes. "I'll love you forever, Nancy," I said, projecting my voice to the audience. They didn't repeat this back in unison, but I could tell they wanted to—they loved her, and they would have loved her even more if they had known what she had done to our play. Mr. Pritchard, by now, had a soft spot for her, I was sure. How could you argue with her now? The crowd was mesmerized, and she was crying and smiling—I had surprised her, and it had been a good surprise, I could tell.

I would never again hold Christina as I did then. (Two days after the play was over, after we'd struck the sets and returned the costumes and prepped the gym for the indoor soccer tour-

nament—that was part of the Drama Club's responsibility—
Christina left town. The weather was making her parents
crazy—they were the type to romanticize Maine because of
visits in the summer, when the breezes were warm and the
days were long.) Our bodies were pressed together, my eyes
level with her neck, my arms around her waist, both of us
cheating a bit toward the audience so they could hear it all—
at this point, they didn't want to miss a thing—and she would
never again say to me what she said then, before the curtain
fell and the crowd erupted in deafening applause. Did it matter that this was a onetime shot, and that she was an actress,
playing a part? Not a bit. In the moment, she meant it, I was
sure. You wait for that—and you wait and you wait. You're
ready when it comes.

"Oh, baby," she said, combing her hand through my hair.
"I'll love you forever, too."

[FINCHES]

I MET DAYNA DURING MY SHORT STINT WORKING FOR THE
veterinarian Stanley Perez. Stanley provided a delivery service
for his clients, and I drove Stanley's truck, returning healed
animals to their owners. We did a lot of large-animal work, lots
of cows. I wore a uniform, white coveralls with a zipper from
the crotch to the neck and the words STAN THE ANIMAL MAN
over the breast pocket. I had a radio, too, clipped to my side. I
had held other jobs requiring uniforms—I'd worked at a Speed
Lube, and as the mate on an island ferry, and as a prep cook at
Robey's Family Restaurant in Springdale. But I felt that wearing a uniform while driving a truck put me in a different
league. I was the master of valuable cargo, I had a flexible
schedule, I was identifiable as a man with places to go, a man
with a distinct and enviable purpose. I was impatient with the

animals, and wary of them, but otherwise, I thought the job was aces.

I didn't know Dayna, but I was bringing her bird back. It was a parakeet which had been treated for parasites, and I had it in a cage on the seat beside me in Stanley's rig. Typically, I'd have hung the cage from a hook in the back of the truck, but at lunchtime I'd filled the back with finches. They were flitting around, uncaged.

Dayna lived out the Sligo Road, in the sardine factory, a three-story chalk-colored building with a service elevator. Stanley told me she was from New York City, which meant a sardine factory apartment was the perfect place for her. You move up to Maine from a city like New York and you want to be reminded every second of where you are. There are many ways to do this: move next to a hockey rink, or across the road from a chicken farm, or within earshot of a sawmill. All of these options are available in Point Allison. But Dayna wanted to see the ocean, so she lived on the third floor of the sardine factory, where the bosses' offices had once been—the landlord had taken out the walls, and through six-foot-high south-facing windows you could see the Royal River widen into the bay.

It had been raining for three days, but now the sky was clearing, the mist had risen, clouds were gathering and rolling away to the east. I parked by the old loading dock at the factory, which hadn't been used in years—lupine sprouted through cracks in the concrete platform. I sat in the quiet of the truck, letting the sun heat the side of my face. When I closed my eyes, I heard the parakeet scratching and fumbling in its cage, which I'd covered with a black felt blanket so as not to upset him in transit. The noises made me want to get the delivery over with, so I walked around to the passenger side and hefted the sphere cage in both arms. The service elevator was just inside the factory's back entrance. When I stepped in and closed its metal gate, the bird spoke.

"Up and down," it said.

"I suppose you think you know where you are," I said.

"Up and down," said the bird.

"I mean, that's really great, you can sense where we are even though you can't see."

The bird's wings clicked against the cage. I waited for it to say something else, imagining its expression under the black cloth, resolute and aloof.

"Okay, fine," I said.

People loved getting their pets back. Like a magician, I removed the cloth when Dayna answered the door. "Oh, Winston, look at you. You're a healthy little beast," she said.

"Winston, Winston, Winston, Winston," said Winston.

These are the differences I see between city women and women from Maine: city women eat vegetables, they can't drive in snow, and they're used to witnessing human indecencies of the public kind rather than the more horrifying private kind. Dayna was definitely from a different part of the world, despite her baseball cap, her bare feet, her tan arms. She moved in a practiced way; she was used to being watched. There was no hesitation in her gestures, nothing wild or desperate.

The apartment looked like a yard sale—it seemed she had no interest in putting things away.

"Oh, if you have a minute, you probably know a lot about this," she said. I was still holding Winston's cage as Dayna walked from the door to the window in her kitchen. There was a hole the size of a hockey puck in the screen. She raked at it with her fingers. "I'm having problems with my squirrels."

And that was another thing: there was an immediate familiarity; she spoke to me as though she knew me. That's from the city. She spoke to me as though she knew my name, knew my brothers, knew about the trouble I'd had with amphetamines in high school, and that nevertheless I'd made it to college, and that there I'd desired women but hadn't had much luck with them.

"I'm Jim," I said.

"Dayna," she said, and she put out her hand, so I propped the cage on my thigh and grabbed her fingers awkwardly. "Here's the problem. I started feeding them, and now they've chewed through my window screen. They even come inside to pee. I came back one afternoon and found a puddle on the counter, like motor oil. They must be sick, don't you think? And they eat everything. They eat my soap and my ant traps and my paper towels."

"You shouldn't have fed them," I said.

"But they expect it now."

"Who cares? That's not your problem."

"But it's my fault they expect it," she said.

"No," I said. "Just stop feeding them." I felt very confident in this.

"What about that?" she asked, pointing at the hole in the screen.

"Rat traps," I said. "That'll do it."

"You're a veterinarian?" she asked.

"I drive the truck," I said.

Winston was glancing at me, craning his neck, then looking away, moving in that twitchy, nervous way birds do. I set the cage down, resting it against Dayna's refrigerator. The job made me hate animals; they were always disapproving and disappointed with me. When they judged, they judged harshly. Those who spend only fleeting time with animals don't notice the judgment—when you have a pet, a pet you feed and speak to in baby talk, it appears to love you. In my daily contact with anonymous animals, though, I learned otherwise. I found that animals have the same deep-seated resentments, the same nagging sense of failure that people do. They have less fear, less shame, but they are equally petty, equally irrational and loathsome.

"Rat traps?" said Dayna. "But they've been like my pets. I just want to get them to behave."

"They're taking advantage of you, Dayna," I said.

She stared at the hole in the screen and bent the frayed strands back to smooth its edges.

Before Dayna there was Andrea, when I worked at Robey's in Springdale—we'd fool around in the walk-in cooler. I'd be sitting on a milk crate and she'd sit in my lap; we'd kiss, she'd bite my ears, then she'd pull down her black uniform pants and I'd pull down mine and she'd say *Will you park the pink Cadillac?* and I would say yes. But I always felt as though she was very far away. I had no idea what we were doing together. We didn't seem to have any real interest in each other at all. We'd gone to see *The Karate Kid* and she'd fallen asleep. She spent all her extra money on cocaine, which only made her nostalgic. Then she left town; she moved to Tucson without saying goodbye. Not long afterwards, I got fired. Robey caught me taking a nap behind the restaurant, out by the dumpsters.

"Could you help me hang Winston's cage?" asked Dayna.

"My pleasure," I said.

Stanley rarely checked up on me, and when he did—by radio—I would sometimes claim engine trouble if I was behind in the delivery schedule, if I'd been wasting time. There were days when I took two-hour picnics on the rocks under the Point Skyler Bridge. Stanley was getting somewhat suspicious. He questioned me more, which made me more interested in fucking off during the workday. That's a problem I have, generally speaking: if people expect me to disappoint them, I'll do my best to meet their expectations.

"I had it in the bedroom, but I guess I could change that," said Dayna.

"Oh, yes," I said. "Definitely."

"You don't think I should have it in the bedroom?"

"Doesn't the bird talk a lot?"

"But I like how Winston talks," she said.

"Winston, Winston, Winston, Winston," said the bird.

But then I noticed the progress I'd made. Dayna wasn't looking at me, just quickly meeting my eye, then turning away, toward Winston, or toward the floor. This was a foothold. She was acting less urban, less fluid; I saw a glimmer of loneliness; I saw her on a Sunday morning listening to the

radio and content to be in this new town (which was all I'd
ever known), looking at the mouth of the harbor, watching the
lobstermen steam eastward, toward the outer islands, thinking, *This is good, this is just what I needed*—when in fact what she
needed was *me*.

Winston's movement had caused the cage to roll quietly
against a pile of jackets in the kitchen doorway. He had left
his trapeze perch, which was upside down, and he was clutching the bottom of the cage. He looked miffed.

"Do you have an extra hook? We could hang the cage right
in the corner of the living room," I suggested.

"What about the kitchen? That might be nice. Then I
could talk to him when I cook," she said.

"Well—"

"What?"

"I don't think that's quite what you want to do."

"I have a hanging basket for onions. I could take that down
and use the same hook."

"But it's the kitchen. Doesn't the bird, um . . . have
smells?"

She looked at me like I'd plucked Winston and was spit-
roasting him. "Winston is extremely clean."

My radio crackled. A transmission came through.

"You on there, Jim?" It was Stanley.

I held up a finger of apology to Dayna, then clicked the
talk button, like a pro. "Gotcha, Stanley," I said.

"Where are you?" Stanley asked.

"Out the Sligo Road. Helping that client with her parakeet."

"You buy some finches today?" he asked.

I looked at Dayna while resting my finger gently on the talk button.

Stanley came through again. "Jim?"

Then I pushed down the button. "I'm not reading you, Stanley. Come again?"

"Finches. You buy some finches at Winkman's earlier today?"

"Finches. Yes, I did. I picked up a few finches earlier today. At Winkman's."

"What's going on, Jim?" asked Stanley.

"Well, Stanley, I'm with a client now. I'm in her kitchen, to tell you the truth. Doing an installation. Putting a cage up. I'll call you back shortly. Over and out."

"In the kitchen?" Stanley asked, but I didn't click back again. "You call me, Jim," he said. "When you're done. Over and out."

"Now I'm curious," said Dayna. She walked to the living room, so I picked up Winston's cage and followed her. She sat on the arm of the couch, and I was towering over her in my coveralls with the cage in my arms.

"Where are they?" she asked.

"They?"

"The finches."

"They're out in the truck," I said. I had always wished to be a better liar, especially with people I was attracted to. It made things easier, it seemed, if you could bend the truth in a smooth and natural way. The problem was, I actually didn't know what I was doing with the finches. I wasn't sure why I'd bought them. I was at Winkman's, picking up a case of cat toys for Stanley, when I'd seen the birds— the kind which sit on telephone wires—Winkman had a new walk-in cage full of them. Winkman's is this dark place, lit mostly by neon fish tanks, but I could see the birds clearly, they were the size of those large marshmallow peanuts, and they were fluttering their wings against each other, angry about their predicament, somewhat confused. Edgy. Jerking their swivel heads at notched increments, as though in constant disbelief. They made me nervous.

"Hey, hey! It's Stan the Animal Man," Winkman had said. The guy was an asshole. He was a hippie, but for no better reason than that it allowed him to be careless and lazy. He had a mangy beard and kept a boa constrictor draped over his shoulders. He called the snake Bootsie.

"Jim," I said. "It's Jim, not Stan."

"You're gonna be a vet, though, right, Jimmy? Jimmy the Animal Man? You'll take over when Stan's done?"

"No," I said. We'd been through this before. "I need some cat toys."

Winkman stroked the snake. *Yes*, Winkman seemed to say, *I have a twelve-foot killer wrapped around my neck, and the killer is my friend, and I can kiss it and call it Bootsie*. I didn't care. He always spoke to me in the chipper voice of a game-show host. I was sure the snake hated Winkman, too, wanted to eat him, and I wished for that.

"Well, we've got squeakers, fuzz balls, rubber mice, furry mice, fuzzy dice, and the Kitty Kong," said Winkman.

"Get me what Stanley usually gets," I said.

"The usual," said Winkman.

The snake raised its head and snapped out its flashy red tongue three times.

"Bootsie," said Winkman. "You gorgeous, gorgeous, beautiful devil. You smell me? Is that what you smell?"

I tried to look as bored as possible.

"Oh, Bootsie," Winkman continued. "My beauty. You're hungry for birds, aren't you? You love them so much, don't you, Boots?" The snake's head rested on the counter. It's skin didn't look shiny enough. I could tell Bootsie thought the both of us were fools.

Winkman passed me a cardboard box. "Will that be all?"

"And twenty finches," I said. "Put them on Stanley's account." For some reason I just needed to get them out of that store.

And now, at Dayna's, I pictured the finches in the truck: they'd calmed down, they'd found places to perch and rest, they were waiting in the dark, preening, rustling their wings.

Winston was clinging to the side of the cage, agitated. He pecked at the zipper of my coveralls.

"Winston! Be nice," said Dayna.

"Winston, Winston," said Winston. Then he went back at it.

Dayna walked to the kitchen and returned with a large screw-in hook and a pair of pliers.

"Let's put it in here," she said. "You're probably right about the kitchen." She kicked us a path to the corner of the room, clearing aside stray sneakers, bags of cat litter, and coffee-stained Styrofoam cups.

She carried two chairs to the corner, and I stood on one

with the cage in my arms and she stood on the other, installing the hook.

With her arms reaching above her head, I looked at her breasts, and she glanced down and caught me looking, and I looked up at the hook. We both looked at the hook. When it was ready, sunk deep in the ceiling, I steadied my feet on the chair and lifted the cage from my chest to eye level. As Dayna used the pliers to try to catch the cage's handle on the hook, Winston was staring me down.

"Hurry," I said.

"I'm trying," she said.

I looked at Dayna through the bars of the cage. She held a stubborn, determined look while working to get the handle in place; her eyes narrowed.

Winston was making his unsteady way toward me, clutching a horizontal bar in one claw and a vertical one in the other, shuddering his wings for balance. His beak approached my nose.

"Oh . . . crap . . ." I said.

"Almost there," she said.

Winston cocked his head to the side, then came at me. I turned my cheek to the bird, and his beak bumped against it. I was holding my breath.

"Got it," she said, and I let go, pushing away from Winston and losing my footing. When I hit the floor, one of my ankles turned and I landed on my ass. Dayna looked down, confused, and there was a beat of silence, then the cage—and Winston— was moving quickly toward me. I took it hard on the chest.

"Oh!" cried Dayna.

Winston and I didn't speak. The hook had ripped through

the plaster. He was flying as best he could inside the sphere. He flapped and flapped, furious. The cage had knocked the wind from me.

"Jeez, I'm sorry," she said.

There was a pain in my ribs when I took a breath and I felt a burn on my chin, but I tried to motion that I was okay.

"No, really, you must be hurt," she said. "Oh, man, you're bleeding." She looked genuinely upset as she climbed down and ran to the bathroom.

It's funny: I take the fondness I remember, the good feelings I have about her, and I think about walking into her kitchen then, the wind knocked out of me, looking for a glass of water. I remember the empty box of instant spuds on her electric range, the sink full of crusty plates, every cabinet and drawer open. I have a general, queasy feeling of regret when I think of it now, not for the particulars—I couldn't find a clean cup, didn't want to rummage further, so I moved quietly back out to the living room—but for the whole thing, falling in love with her, the beginning, the end. The end.

She taped an oversized gauze pad to my chin, and she propped Winston's cage on the ground in the corner, with a bag of cat litter wedged against it so it wouldn't roll.

"Little beast," I said.

"Winston, Winston, Winston, Winston," said Winston. I imagined the bird on the shoulder of a pirate, chatting away while I walked the plank.

Dayna took an armload of laundry off her couch for me, and she sat against the wall, on a pile of magazines.

"How did you get this job?" she asked.

"You know how things are around here," I said, stupidly.

"No I don't," she said.

"Everyone knows everyone," I said. "Stanley thought I was the right one for the job." In the corner of my eye, I saw a squirrel, which I thought at first was a cat—its gray tail rose from behind a stack of World Books. "Look," I said. Dayna turned around. "Here they are again." she said. She shifted her weight, and the magazines loosened beneath her, spilling over on both sides.

It froze and looked at us. I felt my stomach chill. I reached inside my breast pocket for my tape measure, which I cocked back in my throwing hand, and looked at Dayna. "Okay?" I asked her. She said nothing, but she nodded, grimly. I fired the tape measure at the squirrel. It thudded against the far wall, leaving a cracked pockmark in the plaster, and the squirrel flinched but held its ground.

Dayna and I looked at the squirrel, and the squirrel returned our gaze, fiercely, with its black marble eyes. Dayna had her back against the foot of the couch now. We stared in silence. I was sitting on the couch, with my hands on my knees, and her shoulder was just inches from me. I lifted my hand and pressed the back of it against her arm, trying to get her attention, but she didn't turn around, she was watching the squirrel. I thought this was very weird, that she wasn't turning around, and that I wasn't taking my hand away.

"Hey," I said, and the squirrel left its post, returning to the kitchen. "Do you want to go for a ride in the truck?"

She turned and scrunched her eyebrows at me. "Not so much. Why?"

"I was thinking I could show you around," I said.

"Why did you buy those birds, anyway?" she asked. "Really."

"You go to Winkman's, then you'll know. The guy's a criminal."

"Are you going to keep them at your house?" she asked.

"Probably," I said. But I needed a cage, and I didn't really want them around. I just hadn't liked the idea of Winkman's snake eating them. It's not as though I was saving them—who knows if I could treat them any better—I was just acting on a strong urge to get them out of Winkman's reach.

"Well, I can't go now, if that's what you're asking," she said.

"Have you been over to Soper Island?" I asked.

"Nope," she said.

"Well, you've got to go," I said.

"Do I? Why's that?" she asked. She was like that.

"Well," I said. "It's worth it. I promise."

"I'd need to be back by seven," she said.

"No problem. We'll do a quick loop," I said.

It seemed to be a really tough decision for her. "All right," she said, finally.

I radioed Stanley.

"Hey, boss," I said.

"Where are you?" asked Stanley.

"I've got to run a quick errand, then I'll be back. Go ahead home, if you want. I'm off the clock."

"I want to talk to you, Jim," he said.

"See you tomorrow, Stanley," I said, and I clicked off the radio.

My problem has always been anticipation. I expect the best, and I expect the worst. The bad part is the expecting. Even then, as I radioed Stanley, I looked at Dayna—a real beauty, the kind that makes you hurt, makes you want to apologize—and I saw my future. Attachment. Pain. Things being thrown at me in a motel room at four in the morning.

Later, on the Point Skyler Bridge, driving north toward the cliffs near Soper Island, I glanced at Dayna in the passenger seat, and I watched her as she stared at the view. What she was looking at was the best vista in all of Point Allison. I was proud she liked it. The light at that time of day was perfect, so I put on my hazards, slowed to a stop, and snapped the air brakes. From that spot exactly you could see the water white against the rocks on Soper, then the green shallows, then the deep black water in the middle of the channel. And of course everywhere else, spruce and pine trees. The air was cool but the sun was still warm. The cars behind me honked, and a pickup truck clipped by us and its driver told me to fuck myself. I asked Dayna to come with me to the rear of the truck, and there I clicked open the padlock, hopped on the bumper, and grabbed the nylon strap to pull open the door. I hesitated. Then I looked at Dayna. She stood tentatively with her arms folded, no smile. But this fact remained: she was there, with me, waiting. After pulling open the door, I jumped from the bumper, landing beside her, and put my hand on her arm, and when I kissed her, the gauze pad brushed her chin. Her lips didn't move and she frowned. "Hey," she said. "The finches."

The sun was just below the trees on Point Skyler. Wind blew from the south, whistling by the bridge towers. Cars sped around us on the left. The interior of the truck was in shadows; we couldn't see a thing. Nothing burst from the truck. We looked in silence.

Then they came, all of them, in uneven rows—much tinier, it seemed, than when I'd bought them—they hopped from the darkness to the bumper. One after the next they dropped in a brief free fall from the truck, caught the updraft, and vanished through the suspension cables. They dipped under the bridge, or shot north up the river, too quick to see.

I wanted another chance to watch them, but it was over, they had all flown away.

A YEAR AFTER WE BROKE UP, I ATTENDED A WEDDING IN Bangor and Dayna was there. I'd never seen her in heels. She was nearly as tall as I was, and not having talked to her for all that time—well, she looked perfect. She was wearing glasses, and her eyes were cold.

I approached her after three glasses of beer. She was sitting on a white plastic chair at the edge of the tent, alone, having a cigarette away from the crowd.

"Hiya," I said.

"Hi," she said.

"Great band, huh?"

"Sure," she said.

You see, I'd been the one to cut things off, which is to say I'm fairly brain dead when it comes to staying happy. With a good enough ramp, just about anyone can jump twelve buses on a motorcycle. Sticking the landing, though—that's something else entirely.

I said, "Listen, Dayna, we both know I'm the one who messed it all up—"

She rolled her eyes.

"I could apologize. I have apologized, and it's crap. I know," I said.

"Jim, are you drunk?" she asked.

"The thing is, we were so close."

"Yes, we were."

"And I haven't even talked to you in a year."

"Nope."

"Isn't it crazy? We have two years together, we're together almost every day, and then zilch. Nothing. Total strangers. What I mean is—"

"What?"

"I miss knowing you."

She scrunched up her nose. "Why should that matter?"

I thought about that one. The best part had been the beginning, when everything was unknown. I wasn't proud of that. "How's Winston?" I asked.

"Winston? He's gone. I released him off the bridge," she said.

"Really?"

"No, you dope. Not really."

"Winston's still around?"

"Yes." She was smirking; she seemed pleased with herself.

"Can we dance?" I asked.

"Jesus," she said, and shook her head.

"Well, come on. Just a dance."

"As long as you shut up. No more talking."

"Agreed," I said.

People were filtering out of the tent to smoke cigarettes and look at the stars. It was a warm night with a breeze. Dayna really looked fantastic. We didn't hold hands. We faced each other, not dancing, just swaying there, sometimes bumping into other dancers. She looked over my shoulder, and I couldn't read her eyes at all. When the song ended, I touched her arm and had a flash of hope, thinking we'd get back together, but it must have just been the feeling of not knowing her at all.